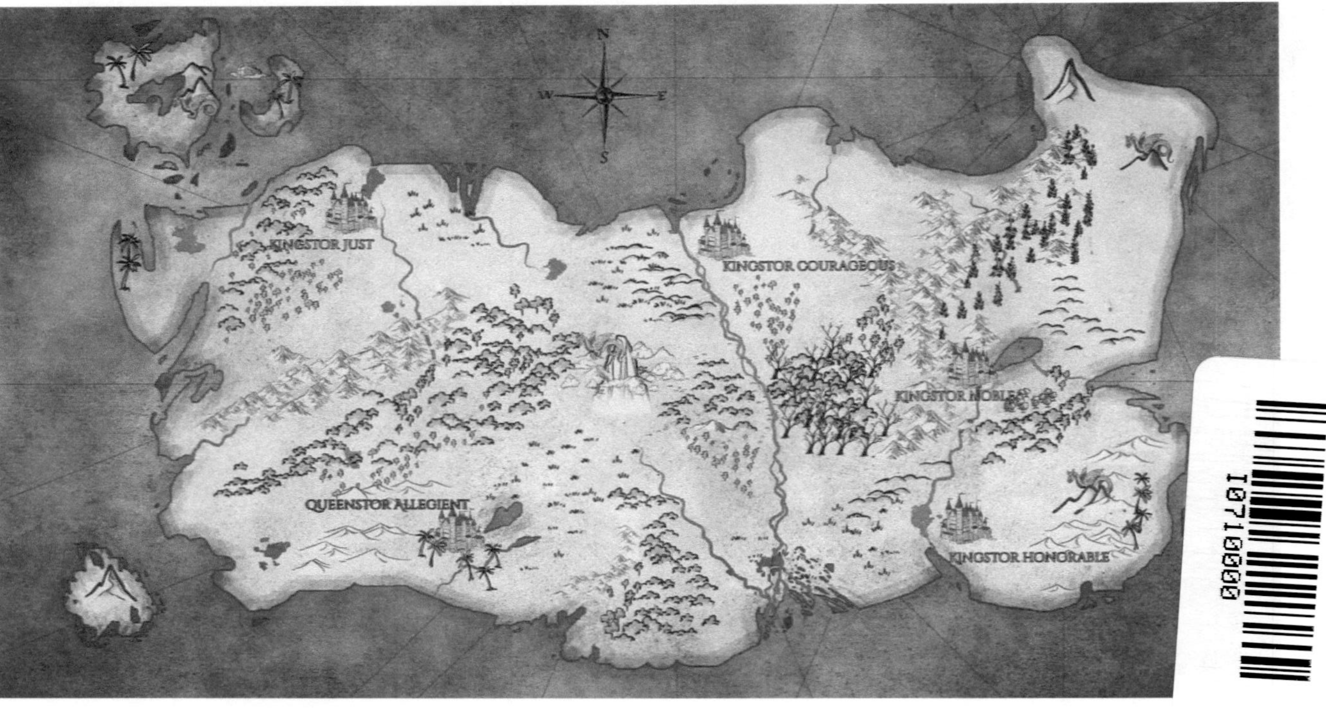
N
W
E
S
KINGSTOR JUST
KINGSTOR COURAGEOUS
KINGSTOR NOBLE
QUEENSTOR ALLEGIENT
KINGSTOR HONORABLE

THE HEART OF AVONOA

<u>Avonoa Series</u>
The Secret of Avonoa (Book One)
The Shadow of Avonoa (Book Two)
The Heart of Avonoa (Book Three)
The Traitor of Avonoa (Book Four)
The Krusible of Avonoa (Book Five)

Also by author HRB Collotzi:

<u>Dragons of Avonoa Series</u>
The Gatekeeper of Death (Book One)

<u>The People of the Storm Series</u>
People of the Storm
People of the Storm 2

THE HEART OF AVONOA

HRB COLLOTZI

AVONOA SERIES BOOK THREE

ISBN: 978-1-962628-16-7
Library of Congress Control Number: 2019915045
Published by HRB Collotzi
Rosemount, Minnesota

www.avonoa.com

This book is dedicated to my parents!

Mom, thank you for your love and support every step of the way on the journey of writing these books! Thank you for teaching me that everything is possible! I love you!

Dad, thank you for always being there to help me with my questions and teaching me so much! Thank you for teaching me to be a strong woman! I love you!

Both of you, together, separate, and in your different ways, made me the woman I am today! You both helped make these books a reality!

CONTENTS

1

A NAME AND A BLESSING

"You know, it's supposed to be a sign of trouble when a black dragon hatches in the middle of the day." Sunlight spilled across the rich blue of the female dragon's back, making the cavern dazzle. A scratching sound came from in front of her.

"I've heard that," the large gray dragon answered. He lay curled around a teardrop-shaped midnight-black rock. It could easily have been mistaken for a large black gem, but because of its engorged size, any dragon would know it was a fertilized dragon egg. And by the size of it, ready to hatch at any moment. "If he's anything like you, he should pop out any minute," he chortled. The scratching grew louder.

She lifted her slim head off the floor. "I didn't see you complaining when you offered me your heart," she teased back. "Besides, I'm not that bad, am I?"

He chuckled again and readjusted himself around the black egg. Its many facets caught the light and made the cavern sparkle even more. "I've never met a dragon so inherently immune to following directions."

She laid her head back down. "It's a good thing he'll have you here to teach him. You are so good with young ones." She sighed, "I can't believe we're going to have our own."

He snorted, "I can't believe you gave up the chance to order me about some more."

After a quiet lull, the egg shook violently. "Almost time now." The gray dragon stood up from his vigilant warming position. "Ah," he groaned as he stretched his sinewy neck and spread his claws out to their full extent. "You're aware that we won't have a moment's peace for a long time around here," he said, extending his hind legs before loping over to join the dame.

"Since when has it ever been peaceful in here?" she growled playfully, allowing him to curl around her.

The pair lazed a while longer while watching the egg shake and rattle in its divot. Finally, when the noise built to its paramount, they raised their heads and stretched their necks to await the moment of breech.

"You know what you're going to name him?" he whispered.

"Of course I know," she whispered back.

Neither of them noticed the shadow appear behind them in the opening of the cave.

The egg vibrated ferociously, then shuddered to a stop. A hairline crack appeared on the left side of the point at the top and slowly spread down to the rounded bottom. Without warning the two sides burst apart, throwing egg shards in every direction. The new parents flinched at the sudden appearance of their offspring before slow smiles spread across their mouths. The dame took a breath and opened her maw, but too late.

"Dakoon," a voice said from the entrance of the cave.

The dame's eyes widened at the shock of hearing someone else's voice. Then the weight of what it had said dawned on her. She sprang toward the voice, loosing a torrent of flame to fill the entrance.

"HOW DARE YOU NAME MY SON!!" she roared at the figure engulfed in flame.

"Calm yourself, Niktiya." The flame died down to reveal the prophetess Visi. Her dull white scales looked almost as beautiful as they had in her youth as the sunshine behind her ricocheted off them. But the light did nothing to hide her hideous, drooping eyes. "That's what you were going to name him anyway." Her raspy voice filled the cavern. "I've come to give him a name—" she turned her eyes on the new hatchling, "and a blessing."

Niktiya's anger faded into surprise. "A blessing?" she asked. "You haven't given any hatchling a blessing for decades."

"Almost a century," the prophetess corrected her, "but this hatchling will be special." She crawled toward him with a limp in her step. "Tustan," she acknowledged the father without looking at him.

"Prophetess," he mumbled as he slunk out of her way.

A rumble began in the bottom of Visi's throat. It grew in pitch as it became louder. Soon she hummed. "This hatchling will grow to be strong and brave. Many lives, alone, will he save," the old dragon dame chanted. "Black like the night and swift like his mother. Bold and smart like no other." The two parents watched in nervous anticipation. The wizened old dragon lifted her claw over his head. As the little dragon shuffled around in the broken remnants of his egg, the prophetess sprinkled something from her grasp onto him. She mumbled something inaudible, even for a dragon with sensitive hearing. Then, replacing her claw on the ground, she looked at the new parents with a stern gaze. "Broken heart only when the time is right, for it shall be to end a fight. So I say so let it be, this dragon blessing all shall see."

2

IRRITATIONS

"It would be easier, yes." Visi sat curled on the ground as Priya paced along the rocky ridge of the cliff face. The old seer dragon's drooping white scales, once brilliant, sagged over the ledge above the precipice beside her. This location would be extremely difficult for a human to attain, which made it a perfect place for dragons to meet. "But since when has Hiro ever done anything easy?"

Priya's sharp green scales sparkled in the warm spring sunlight as she stared out over the landscape. The tip of Teardrop Sea sprawled off to the east. The Forest of Shenharah stretched on the horizon in front of them. A little Hamees village and several other human villages lay nestled somewhere amidst the trees and hills of the northern part of the Noble Kingdom they surveyed from this perch. On the south side of the mountains behind them, Kingstor Noble's great castle lay, built in the shadow of these mountains. Far in the distant north, too far for even dragon eyes to see from where Priya stood, The Great Northern Mountain reached out to scratch at the sky.

"But if I could—" Priya started again.

"No," Visi's gravelly voice was firm as she rose. Why did getting old have to hurt so much? The pain was an insult. "It won't happen, so don't dwell on it. I'm not saying you shouldn't try, but don't be disappointed when it doesn't work. Now," the old dame asked as Priya turned to face her, "do you remember what it looks like?"

"Of course I do." The young green dragon shook her head indignantly and turned away.

"Do you remember what to say?"

"You know I do."

"Don't forget to bring the praxen seeds—"

"I know."

"—and the foolsberry the second day—"

Priya nodded.

"—and the signal at the exact time."

Priya's head dipped.

Visi sighed. She could see the weight on the little green dragon's shoulders. She could see the anxiety in her eyes. She stepped next to her and matched her position, sitting back on her haunches.

"If it's any help," she whispered, "one way or another, it will all be over soon."

Priya nodded again.

"You've done so well, little one," Visi's voice shook. "You will kill him soon."

———

Three sets of dragon claws clattered on the rocks outside of Rakgar's lair. One set was brown with an orange tinge; one, the light gray of a stormy sky; and the last, black as a starless night.

"Hiro, Tog, you go first," the brown dragon grumbled to the other two. "If I set a claw in there before you, he'll think I've come without you and I'll be ash before either of you pass the entry."

"He's that bad, Trakillyn?" the black dragon questioned.

"Hiro, you've no idea," Trakillyn answered. "You're a favorite of his. He's kinder to you than he is to anyone else. Yet—"

A deafening roar exploded from the cave along with a burst of flame, making all three dragons jerk back.

"Oh, spit in Tarsa's eye," Trakillyn muttered, stumbling backward. "I think I'll just stand guard out here a minute." Easing back on his haunches, the long spikes on his shoulders faced the rocks to one side of the cave entrance and his nose pointed up at the magnificent mountains floating around the even more imposing Inner Mountain on which the three had landed. His tail twitched from nerves and his wide eyes likely didn't even see the clear spring sky and setting sun.

"Well, Tog," Hiro turned to the gray dragon with short ridges running down his spine, "I suppose it wouldn't be wise to keep him waiting."

Hiro and Tog entered the cave together. "He gets worse every day," Tog, Hiro's best friend, grumbled next to him. Tog scrubbed smoke out of his protruding eyes as an orange dame scurried out of the cave opening they had come through and took off into the air. They wondered if she was the cause of the frightening roar. "He sent Trakillyn and Sanatab to cut down fifty oak trees," Tog whispered once she had gone. "He gave no reason. He sent Makki to stack them, again with no explanation, he just ordered him. Then he forced Burrabill and Hakkil to carry the same trees into the Black Forest and leave them there. No explanation, and ordering them around like a human king. Like he has the authority." Their claws beat a rhythm against the stone as they walked through the cave toward Rakgar's lair. Tog lowered his voice even more in the silence, ensuring that only Hiro could hear him. "He told Makki not to tell anyone and insisted on his wyrd. The only reason I know any of this is because I stumbled upon Makki while he was at it. And this happened in just the last sun cycle," Tog finished out of the corner of his maw. They approached Rakgar, their leader, and he turned to acknowledge them.

Hiro and Tog bobbed their heads, but Hiro spoke. "Clear skies to you, Rakgar. You summoned us?"

"Where is Trakillyn?" Rakgar bellowed, making the horns and barbels jutting from his head bristle in anger. Those horns traced paths down his back and shoulders and onto the backs of his front legs. All of them seemed to spike higher with the big dragon's rage. Rakgar's head was almost as large as Hiro's body. He was a threatening figure to the entire ruck, except perhaps Hiro.

Hiro and Tog shared a glance. "I asked him to stand guard," Hiro said. "I thought we might not want to be disturbed."

Rakgar followed Hiro's eyes to the others surrounding them in the cave. There weren't many that chose to spend time in Rakgar's lair these days. Seeing how Rakgar was twice the size of all the larger dans, his temper was best to avoid. Only Milah and Mitashio and a faerie woman named Skorkot lingered.

Milah and Mitashio, a pair of brown brothers from the same egg, had always despised Tog and Dakoon, as Hiro had formerly been known. There was no specific reason for the animosity, but it emanated from both sides. Hiro was known for being a rather good-looking dan. Since he only had two gracefully, curving horns on his head and nowhere else, some said he looked feminine. The dames, however, thought him extremely handsome.

No matter the cause of the enmity, the brothers had sought a confidence with Rakgar as soon as Hiro began disagreeing with their leader. Hiro's father Tusten, Rakgar's most trusted counselor, had died several months ago. It was then that Hiro began to disagree more often with Rakgar, so to ingratiate themselves, Milah and Mitashio had become his Yes-Dragons.

"Milah and Mitashio know of your assignment," Rakgar rumbled in his deep, sonorous voice. "Did you discover anything?"

"No, Rakgar," Hiro answered.

"We searched the area that I last visited with Priya, Rakgar. There's still no sign of your daughter," Tog said cautiously. From the random place where Tog and Priya had landed in the forest, a short distance from the Rock Clouds in which they lived, Priya had disappeared. What Tog and Hiro didn't tell Rakgar is that Princess Anna, a human princess, had appeared at that time. Anna had tricked Tog into bringing her to the Rock Clouds and they left before Priya could return. "We found nothing more than the necklace I returned to you three sun cycles ago. I saw her tracks in the ground, but nothing more. No ash, no weapons, nothing."

"I've searched the area as well, Rakgar," Hiro supported his friend. "She's nowhere to be found. There are no fresh tracks to follow. She must have flown away."

Smoke drifted from Rakgar's nostrils as his spikes bristled again. Hiro and Tog shared another uneasy glance before Hiro took a step forward. "I'm sure she's fine, Rakgar," Hiro edged toward the massive dragon. "We also found no blood, or embers, or anything to indicate she's been harmed. We ranged well away from the point she disappeared to the place where—" Hiro cut himself off quickly. He'd almost said, "where Tog found Anna." Instead, he finished with, "—where Tog decided to come back."

"We left burns and upward slashes on the trees," Tog quickly added to cover Hiro's slip. "We left the signs to come home and I'm sure she'll return when she finds them."

Rakgar snorted and shot flame from his nostrils. Both Hiro and Tog flinched at the sudden threat. Rakgar's brows lifted and he straightened from his crouch, noticing their hesitation. Even Milah and Mitashio turned aside ever so slightly from their leader. All the dragons feared Rakgar's anger, but the faerie Skorkot, with silver hair pouring down her back and transparent skin pulsing with her blood, stood staring boldly at the dragons.

Rakgar's eyes noted the dragons' movement. "Are you afraid of me, Hiro?" Rakgar almost whispered, but it didn't sound like a concern.

Hiro couldn't meet his eyes. "I fear your disappointment, Rakgar. I'm disappointed at Priya's continued absence as well, but…"

"But what, Hiro?" Rakgar growled.

"Many—" Hiro shrugged, "—many say your anger is irrational."

Rakgar snorted again, but in Tog's direction this time. "Do they?"

Tog hung his head and twitched it to several different positions to avoid eye contact. With toggling eyes that could see in two different directions at once, it was an undertaking for him.

When Rakgar's mouth started to open again, Hiro hurried forward to position himself between Tog and the leader. "It's understandable to be upset when your daughter goes missing. I'm angry as well. And while our anger may not be rational, we can't control being upset by something like this."

The corner of Rakgar's lip curled in amusement. "You think I'm upset about a wayward daughter? Well, it's not the first time she's disappointed me." Rakgar turned his back long enough for Hiro and Tog to share another glance, this time laced with confusion. When Rakgar settled back on the floor he waved his claw to Milah and Mitashio. "Tell them," he said to the brothers.

Milah stepped forward. His back straight, he looked down his triangular snout at the black and gray dragons. "You've heard the rumors of dragons being killed on the surface?" When Hiro and Tog nodded, he continued. "That's only a fraction of the truth. Several dragons—"

"—twenty-three to be exact," Mitashio interjected.

"Twenty-three dragons, male and female, have been attacked by humans in the past fourteen sun cycles. Centaurs have prevented three attacks and in only four instances have any dragons been able to escape with their hides."

"Five from the—" Mitashio started but Milah finished, as he usually did.

"Five from the Ice Ruck up north, and they have expressed that that is an anomalously high number for them. They haven't had a clash with humans in over four centuries, and we haven't clashed in…"

When Milah snaked his head around to look at his brother for an answer, Mitashio sat up straighter. "Ever," he answered.

Milah nodded and returned his condescending gaze to Hiro. "Our ruck has lived in the Rock Clouds for over six centuries and has never had a single death from human contact until you, Hiro Tekla feira Dakoon, recklessly abandoned your home and our laws—" Milah's voice rose to a yell in an attempt to cover Hiro's voice.

"I'm a fully accepted member of this ruck—" Hiro yelled back in defense.

"You're a blood traitor slug!" Mitashio hollered.

"You have no right to pass judgment—" Tog joined in alongside his friend.

"Go freeze in the Northern Waste!" Milah bellowed.

"Go freeze yourself!" Hiro howled back.

Before any of the attack postures they'd all struck could be put to use, Rakgar's roar echoed from the walls to silence them. Smoke seeped from his nose and mouth as he licked his fangs. "This is the source of my anger," he growled. "Humans are attacking dragons and dragons are attacking each other! There'll be no more of us left to fight if we don't do something about it!" Rakgar paced across the stone floor of the lair. "These humans no longer fear us. They think us weak. A game animal. They think it sport to hunt us." Back and forth across the cave Rakgar's claws beat a rhythm with his tail swaying. "We must strike fear into their hearts. We must remind them how dangerous a dragon can be."

"But Rakgar," Hiro pulled his eyes from Milah's while Milah watched Hiro through narrowed slits, "what can we do? If we fight back at their attacks, humans are bound to see our intelligence. If we organize or help each other in any way—you've said yourself that we can't expose—"

"What do you propose, Rakgar?" Mitashio asked.

"One strike." Rakgar nodded to himself. "No more. You're right, Hiro, many strikes would cause alarm among the humans, but just one…"

"To the heart of the Noble Kingdom," Skorkot finally spoke. Her whisper seemed to have been waiting for this moment.

Rakgar stared at the wall. "We must strike at something precious to the humans. They must fear the dragons again."

When he fell silent, Hiro stepped toward the mighty gray dragon. "Rakgar?" he asked quietly.

Hearing his name, Rakgar spun to face Hiro. He rumbled in the back of his throat and his mouth parted in an evil grin. "You will kidnap their princess."

Hiro's maw fell open and he stumbled backward.

"Wouldn't that be considered an intentional action?" Tog asked from behind Hiro.

Milah shrugged. "Take her when she's outside the castle," he said, as if he kidnapped humans every day. "It can seem random if you plan it right." He took a step forward. "I'll go. If she struggles, I'll eat her in front of them and the humans will fear dragons again, to be sure."

Milah eat Anna? "Rakgar," Hiro closed his jaws and blinked back any sign of fear in his eyes. "I've been to Kingstor Noble. I know the layout of the city and the castle. I know the behavior of the guards as well as the king and the princess." Suppressing his concern for the human woman, Hiro looked into Rakgar's eye. "I have the most reason to attack them. They might even still be expecting it." Tog's eye closest to Hiro narrowed, but Hiro ignored it. "I'll go."

Hiro saw Tog's head droop. Rakgar nodded. "Yes, Hiro, you should be the one to do it. Fly in, take the princess in any way possible, and bring her back here."

"Here?" Hiro's fire guttered. Here? The Rock Clouds? What was Rakgar thinking? Had he returned his mind? "But Rakgar, the law—"

"I know the law, Hiro," Rakgar growled, baring his fangs.

Hiro searched the faces around him, but even in Tog's eyes he found no support. He rolled his shoulder and attempted to soften his heart against the woman. "If I bring her to the Rock Clouds, we couldn't force the entire ruck to be silent while she's here. Someone would speak in front of her."

"And she would die for it," Milah hissed.

Hiro swallowed, blinking at the ground. "Precisely. If a human princess dies in the Rock Clouds having been taken by a dragon, King Philip and his army will march up the mountain and rip it open with their bare hands to find her." He leveled his head with the others', but didn't look at any of them. "What will happen then? Hatchlings won't stay silent in an attack. Their dames and dans will be forced to hunt down and kill every human that hears an utterance and there won't be any assurance they'll find them all. And if dragons are chasing down and killing humans, what stops the other humans from putting together rumors and truth? We can't control the outcome of an invasion of that magnitude." Even Milah seemed pensive. "Perhaps if I take her somewhere else?"

"No," Rakgar growled, "an animal would take her to its home."

"We could return her." Tog's voice was only loud enough for the small party to hear, even if there had been others in the cave. When they eyed him skeptically, he continued. "Even make it look like an escape."

"But someone is bound to speak in front of her," Milah insisted, "Hiro said it himself. We can't control everyone."

After a moment's silence, Rakgar nodded. "I give the human woman an exemption from our law."

Skorkot flashed the first sign of incredulity. She jerked her head so fast her hair whipped against her face. "You give her what?" she hissed.

Hiro's wasn't the only maw hanging at the words. Rakgar stood straight, his enormous claws at rest from their pacing. "The human woman known as Princess Anna of the Noble Kingdom will be the first and only human to be granted an exemption from the Killing Law of dragons. She will be the only human in existence to hear a dragon speak and not be killed for it." Rakgar considered the shocked and bewildered eyes of the dragons around him, but his eyes held no warmth, no mercy; just pure, mad rage. "When she's returned to her home, anyone she tells of dragons speaking will think her mind is gone."

Hiro gathered his wits. "We must return her unharmed, Rakgar. Before King Philip mounts an attack."

"And not a scratch will be on her." He glared down at Hiro. "See to it."

———

Hiro and Tog crawled from the spacious lair. Several dragons waited outside and one voice eagerly greeted them before they could draw a breath.

"Hiro! Tog! What's going on in there?" Prak's nasal tones always sounded strange coming from his small, reddish-brown body that had as many fearsome spikes and horns as Rakgar's did, and twice as many running down his spine, on both sides of it. "All Trakillyn will say is that no one should enter. Is Rakgar angry? What's wrong? Where's Priya? I'm going to ask Rakgar for an assignment too! Are you two going somewhere? Did Rakgar give you an assignment? Were you reporting to him or were you getting an assignment? Or both? Can I come too?"

When Hiro held up a claw to calm the younger dragon, the talking ceased. "Yes, both, Prak. I reported to Rakgar and now he has a private assignment for me." Prak's mouth popped open again, but before another barrage of questions could emit, Hiro hurriedly added, "I must go alone, Prak. I'm sorry."

"But—"

"Hiro," Tog cut in, "perhaps I should go for you. You can show me where to go and maybe I can—"

Hiro shook his head. "What do you fear more, my friend? That I won't return or that I will?"

Tog glanced at Prak, who watched them with a mixture of fascination and calculation. When Tog finally met Hiro's eye, he shook his head. "I fear that when you return, we'll be bound to rename you."

Hiro forced a chuckle. "Don't fear. When I return we'll make Milah and Mitashio bow to Drakkod, the dragon god." Hiro bunched his body, preparing to fly away from the Inner Mountain and the Rock Clouds, but Tog clenched his leg.

With a dangerous glint in his eye, he whispered, "Don't let that creature change you."

Hiro gently pulled Tog's claw away as he said, "Shining days, to you, my friend. I'll return soon."

"Clear skies, to you, Hiro!" Prak called after him. "Return swift and safe!"

Hiro lifted into the air, but didn't angle toward his own lair. Instead, he dipped a wing to the darkening forest beyond the Rock Clouds. Pumping his wings, he glid on a current past the other floating mountain homes of his dragon ruck.

I should be sad to leave, he told himself. *I should be longing for my safe, warm, human-less lair.* But his eyes continued to search the horizon ahead of him.

3

SECRET MEETING

"Why don't you marry her, Torgon?"

Nineteen-year-old Royal General Torgon spluttered into his drink, splashing wine down his chin and onto his plate. While he coughed and wiped his face, Anna muttered, "Gracefully done, Philip."

King Philip, only sixteen upon his coronation several months ago, sat at the head of a small but luxuriously laid dinner table with his sister and Royal General. Princess Anna sat to his right as the closest person to him who could take over the kingdom in a time of need. Royal General Torgon sat on the other side of him, at Philip's left.

"Is it a bad suggestion, Anna?" He observed Torgon—avoiding both of their gazes—through what he hoped were objective eyes. "He's young, strong, loyal, top in the land with a sword, and my best friend. Not to mention, he's a brilliant strategist, knows the laws of the kingdom almost as well as I do, and he's always fair in his dealings. I've never heard a negative word spoken against him from those in his command—I could go on. He's not even ugly!" With that last remark, Torgon jerked the golden fork from his mouth, producing another fit of coughing from his bite of fish.

"Philip," Anna finished her own fish and balanced her fork on the edge of her plate, "I really don't care who you marry me off to. As you said, it is my duty as a Princess of Avonoa to marry the right man for the kingdom. And whoever you choose will be the right man." She lifted her fork again and, although she approached the green beans with apparent ease, a loud CLINK sounded when she stabbed one with a little too much force.

"Well, Torgon," Philip ignored his sister's reaction, "what do you think? You're the only man I could see on the throne should anything happen to me."

Torgon smoothed the napkin on his leg and swallowed. "I don't think I'm the right man for it, Philip."

"Of course, you are!" Philip raised his voice. "Haven't you been listening?"

Philip and Anna stared at Torgon. Torgon smoothed his napkin again, picked up his fork, then set it down. "I just don't think …" He cleared his throat. He picked up his goblet, swirled the wine in it around, but then narrowed his eyes into it with suspicion and put it down as well. "The kingdom needs …" he started, but cleared his throat again.

"I don't think I've ever seen you so out of sorts, Torgon," Philip said, resuming his own meal.

"Well, you put him in the light, Philip," Anna added, sipping her wine. "He probably doesn't want to marry me, but feels he can't refuse."

"Why wouldn't he want to marry you?" Philip mumbled between bites. "You're pretty enough, and he would be next in line for the throne."

"I don't want to be next in line for the throne," Torgon finally spat out.

"Exactly why you would be best for the job," Philip waved him off.

"Perhaps," Anna narrowed her eyes at the Royal General, "he's in love with someone else."

"Ah!" Philip dropped his fork when Torgon's chin angled away from the royal pair. "That must be it. Well done, Anna."

Both Philip and Anna picked up their forks and stared at Torgon while they took their bites. A thick silence hung over the table. One of the servants behind Philip shuffled his feet. A dog barked outside in the distance.

Torgon picked up his fork and knife and tried to cut into a tomato. He cut once, then twice. CLANG! He banged his knife down on the table. "All right!" He sat back and stared at his food without seeing it.

When he finally looked at Philip, the young king simply said, "Confession is not enough." Philip shook his head and stuffed another forkful in his mouth. He and Anna shared a conspiratorial grin.

With a sigh, Torgon resumed the methodical chopping of his food without bringing any to his lips. "I've known her all my life, but nothing will ever come of it. My father didn't know of her before he died, and my mother insists I marry a woman of her choosing from among the wealthy." He paused and then grinned up at Philip. "But I'm not the important one here."

"What do you mean?" Philip asked, his brow creasing. That grin looked dangerous.

"I mean to say," Torgon nodded, "that out of the three of us, perhaps you should focus on finding a queen before dabbling in our love lives." He waved his fork between Anna and himself before pointing at Philip. "You are the king and you should have an heir. Young kings ought to marry quickly, Philip. Wouldn't you agree?"

Anna swiveled her head to look at Philip. "No," he said. He pointed a finger at Anna, then at Torgon. "No. I order both of you to stay out of my love life."

"What love life?" Anna said, turning back to her plate. "Maybe that's why you would see either of us wed before yourself. Maybe you don't have the backbone to face your own circumstance."

"I know my own circumstances better than anyone." He forced himself to take another bite. "Since I currently have no prospects, I think it's important that both of you follow yours.

"And speaking of yours, would you choose this woman over Anna? And the crown?" Philip queried. When Torgon wouldn't meet his eye, Philip's jaw dropped. "Spit in Tarsa's eye—you would." Anna gasped at Philip's curse. Torgon's cheeks spotted with color, but whether from the curse or the revelation, Philip wasn't sure. The king waved both reactions away. "Who is she? Why haven't you told me about her?"

Torgon shrugged. "I told you, she's not wealthy. She's worked in our stables all her life. We grew up together. Philip, you've seen her, after a hunt several years ago. But you wouldn't recognize her even if I could present her to you. Besides, my mother would send her away if she discovered it."

"Well, she has a point," Philip shrugged.

"One minute," Anna's chin jutted out, "are you saying Torgon shouldn't marry the woman he loves just because of her status in life?"

"We are the *Noble* Kingdom, Anna." Philip tore into a hunk of bread. "How would it look if the Royal General married a stable girl?"

"Noble." Anna sat up straighter. "I have seen many servants and commoners commit noble deeds. I see no reason a commoner couldn't act appropriately in front of a king. I, personally, would love to meet her. You should bring her to dinner, Torgon."

"Anna," Philip set down his goblet, "I'm sure such a meeting would make both the woman and Torgon most uncomfortable. She hasn't been trained as a noblewoman."

"Do you even know what it takes to be trained, Philip? 'Pick up this fork,' 'drink with this hand,' 'cross your feet at this angle'…half of it could be taught in a matter of minutes; the other half no one would notice if forgotten. Even the lowliest of stations could come before a king and act respectably, with or without the proper protocol."

"All right, fine." Philip nodded slowly at first, but his enthusiasm grew. "Tomorrow night. Bring her to dinner, Torgon. If nothing else, I would love to see the woman that surpasses Princess Anna in your opinion."

Torgon sighed and pushed his plate away.

———

Hiro could just make out the shape of the grand edifice of Kingstor Noble against the rising sun. Well did he remember the slanted streets disguising an easier path to the castle gates. The glistening dragon-scale rooftops on the wealthier homes; the curved and pointed merlons surrounding the five towers and topping the battlements. Though meant to deter approaching dragons from landing on top of them, Hiro found them particularly intimidating from within the castle courtyard. He should know, as he had once been held prisoner inside that courtyard. From this distance, he couldn't see if the section of the castle he had destroyed in his escape had been repaired yet.

As he soared toward the castle that had once imprisoned him, he found it hard to stop doubting himself and his plan to find the human, Princess Anna.

Perhaps if I just return and say I couldn't find her, he thought for the hundredth time. *Perhaps I really won't be able to get to her.* No! He shook his head and scratched at his shoulder. *What must be done, must be done.*

Unfortunately, no attacks from banshees or scorrands or even a wandering faerie had distracted him from his course along the way. He had made more stops than necessary and even been slow to wake and move on every time. Yet, somehow, he arrived at Kingstor sooner than he'd expected. He had taken his time getting to the

Noble Kingdom, but now renewed his determination to finish his assignment.

Hiro made sure to fly straight through the mountains on the south side of the pass that led to the Hamees village. He might be seen from the village, but he didn't want any other humans to think he came from the Hamees' village, or the villagers might be questioned again about dragons. That could endanger both the Hamees and him.

Odd for a dragon to desire humans to be safe, Hiro thought of his plan. But the Hamees were very different. They were different from other humans as they lived a peaceful life, and they had been kind and protected Hiro when he almost died. He risked exposure by helping them, but they risked everything, including their very way of life, to protect him.

Once he was close enough to be spotted by the castle guards, Hiro lifted his tail to drop, but tilted his wing to sweep wide of the castle. The sun was fully above the horizon by now and glistened on his black scales. He pumped his wings to stay above the king's forest, between the mountains and the castle. He was too far away for any arrows or crossbows to reach him, so he floated past the castle, attempting to seem at ease.

The call of "DRAGON!" could be heard in every direction, echoing from each tower in turn, but Hiro drifted past without turning his head toward the sound. An animal wouldn't understand what they were saying, and this animal wasn't attacking. He was determined to make it seem as if he were just passing through.

He flew over the water behind the castle, where a branch of the Torthoth Mountains encroached against Teardrop Sea. He noted but didn't react to the call of "DRAGON!" echoing from the cliffs next to the water. The king must have a lookout stationed there as well.

There. That should settle a couple of different matters, Hiro thought to himself.

Hiro assumed that King Philip still wondered if the black dragon they had imprisoned was someday going to return and attack. Coming the route he chose, several humans had seen him, but he flew by without bothering anyone. Perhaps that alone would convince the king to ease his attacks on dragons. Also, and more importantly, Anna would know that Hiro was in the area.

Hiro felt the cool air over the water pulling him down, so he pressed his wings against it. Flying level with the castle towers, he couldn't see the other side of Teardrop Sea, but that was his destination. Clear skies and wispy clouds of spring afforded no coverage, so he would be forced to use the distance to circle back around.

Once he was far enough away from the castle, Hiro pumped his wings harder. He circled north, keeping the same distance between himself and Kingstor Noble, hoping no one would expect the dragon to circle back toward them from the north. He knew he could stop in the Hamees village and no one would report it, but he couldn't ask them for help. He didn't want to endanger them any further with his presence.

Hiro and Anna had helped the Hamees men save themselves and their village from a deadly creature just weeks ago. They thought Hiro was a secret pet of Anna's.

While the idea of that irked Hiro, he had to admit to the validity of the excuse. It explained many things for the humans while the truth would put them in grave danger.

Will she come? he thought for the last time. If she didn't come, he would have to think of another way to get to her.

Eventually Hiro flew low over the Hamees village, but he didn't stop. He heard shouts, but they were different from the guards' warning calls. They seemed…joyful. He put it out of his mind and flew to the pass in the mountains connecting the Hamees village to Kingstor Noble. Hiro knew that if Anna came to find him, she would have to pass this way. He ducked into the trees before landing and scuttled behind some boulders to the side.

He curled up on the ground, enjoying the warming dirt beneath his belly. He could hear the Hamees families outside. Small humans squealed and laughed. Hiro had once taught and been taught that humans were brutal to their young. "Beat them or eat them, whatever their fancy." He didn't understand until meeting the Hamees that those teachings weren't true.

He might have even tried to justify those actions, were the teachings true, because the Hamees otherwise lived so peacefully with their oaths of kindness. But some months ago Hiro had seen with his own eyes a human woman place herself between a monster of the earth and her young child. She had sacrificed herself in hopes of saving him. The young child died shortly after his mother did, but that one act brought so many things into question that Hiro had learned all his life. As he lay in his hiding place now, he listened to the humans talking and calling to each other. Increasingly, more of those teachings lay to waste in his mind.

By the time he was in place, the sun had passed its zenith. He watched the road beyond him with keen eyes. He knew he must do all these things in the daytime to put his sharp day vision to use. No human could see him from the road—even with only scant spring buds on the brush—but he would easily see and hear anyone approaching.

He didn't have to wait long. Hiro heard the familiar sound of shod horse hooves clattering on the road. They seemed about as unhurried as he had been when he'd flown past the castle. He listened. It was only one horse, not a carriage or wagon drawn by more. Then he realized that the sound had originated from the village.

Soon enough Jarek came into view, staring intently into the trees. The man's right hand gripped the reins of his horse while the other hung at his side, covered in a brown glove. Hiro's heart twinged at the memory of Jarek's wail when Hiro had burned his hand. It had been necessary though, and the man knew it as well. Their eyes had communicated more than all his speaking with Anna had. Through one look, Jarek had told Hiro to burn the wraith—the creature attacking the humans—and his hand—in order to kill the monster. But even with consent, Jarek's piercing scream still haunted Hiro's mind.

Jarek was part of the Hamees people. A people set apart from other humans. They believed differently and swore sacred oaths to live a peaceful life. Among other oaths, they swore to help others and never lie. These two oaths came in conflict when Anna first asked Jarek not to tell anyone that Hiro was in his barn, and then begged his help to harbor the dragon. Jarek had chosen to help the dragon, which surprised Hiro. From that time on, Hiro assumed the man and the Hamees were anomalies among humans.

As Jarek stared into the trees, the thought was confirmed in Hiro's mind. Jarek must have seen the dragon fly overhead and had actually come to look for it. Did he want to help? Would he try to send it away?

Before he could wonder long, Hiro heard a second set of hooves beating the ground. The second set beat faster and, upon closer inspection, Hiro could tell they came from the direction of Kingstor Noble. Jarek, who had passed Hiro's hiding place by now, heard the approaching rider as well. He shifted his horse to the side of the road to allow the hasty rider to pass, but sat up in his saddle when he saw who approached.

Anna's thick purple riding cloak streamed behind her at her swift pace. Her golden hair whipped around her face when she pulled the reins tight to a halt upon seeing Jarek. The man bowed to her from the saddle.

"Princess Anna," Jarek tucked his left hand behind his back, "I thought I might find you here as well."

"As well?" Anna breathed from exertion, pulling alongside the man's horse. "Who else would you find here?"

"Hiro," Jarek said and nodded toward the trees. "I thought I saw him this morning over the mountains, then half the village saw him over the village just moments ago. Someone told me he dipped down into the trees here."

"He was also seen at the castle," Anna peeked into the forest too, "but only early this morning."

Hiro flipped his tail to the side, thrashing a few bushes with tender spring leaves on them. Both humans turned toward where they heard the sound. Hiro lifted his head from the rocks and trees he hid behind, but still they searched without seeing him. So he allowed a flame to tickle his tongue and slip between his teeth.

Finally Anna pointed. "There! I see him!" She bounced out of her saddle, threw her reins around a branch, and began picking her way through the thick brush. She stopped when she noticed that Jarek wasn't following her. "Are you coming?"

Jarek brought his gloved left hand up to his chest. Turning it over once, he said, "No." He allowed it to fall onto his leg. "You're here now. I only came to see if Hiro needed any help. I probably would have sent a message to you if you hadn't come anyway."

Anna swayed toward the man. "Are you angry with him, Jarek? You know he would never—"

"I know, Anna," Jarek nodded. His hand twitched, but remained on his leg. "I just can't add more moments in my life that I can't explain to others." He lifted his face to her again and heeled his horse in the sides. "It was nice to see you again, Princess Anna. Purity and peace guide you."

"And you." Anna returned the nod and Jarek's horse trotted away.

After Jarek left, Anna took several minutes to complete her struggle through the bushes. When she finally reached Hiro, she planted her fists on her hips. "You couldn't meet me half way?"

"Someone had to watch the road for passersby," Hiro said. She rolled her eyes at him, but he continued. "Besides, if someone came by, they would see us."

The woman's composure softened. "You take a great risk coming here, Hiro. I wouldn't be surprised if my brother sends patrols out to hunt you down. Why would you risk that? What's going on?"

Hiro scratched at the ground. "I've come for you."

Anna's eyes widened and her hands dropped to her sides. "Me? What do you need of me?"

Hiro squinted into the sky. "Well...I've... somewhat...been ordered..."

"Out with it, dragon."

Hiro rolled his shoulder and met her eyes. "I've come to kidnap you."

Anna took a step back, but went no further. "Kidnap me? Why? Who ordered this?"

"Rakgar," Hiro said, but he also moved his head away from her. He didn't want her to feel that he would be violent about fulfilling Rakgar's command.

"Why would he want you to kidnap me?"

Hiro's gaze wandered into the trees toward the Rock Clouds. "He's angry. He claims the cause is the increasing number of attacks on dragons, but I'm certain it's more from—"

Hiro's voice cut off and Anna's eyes narrowed. "From what, Hiro?" She stepped toward the dragon. "You know you can trust me."

"I believe he's angry because his daughter has been missing for months."

"Oh." Anna turned toward the road, pulling her cloak tight around her shoulders.

Hiro wondered if she might make a run for it. "Perhaps I could tell Rakgar that you were too well guarded and I couldn't retrieve you. I could attack the castle to have decent memories to pass to Rakgar."

When the woman faced him again, her jaw was set. "No, that lie would cause even more problems." She shook her head. "You must take me with you. But you can't take me from here. I must be seen in Kingstor again so the Hamees won't be questioned."

Hiro nodded. "Meet me by the waterfall at the edge of the castle wall on the mountains."

"I'll make sure my return to the castle is well known." Anna started back through the trees toward her waiting horse, adding over her shoulder, "I'll be there by nightfall."

4

NOCTURNAL INTRIGUES

"No one has taken the bait?" Philip moved a pawn.

"Not yet." Torgon glared at the game board.

"Perhaps they don't believe you capable."

"Philip," Torgon cast him another tolerant-older-brother-type look, "do you not trust me to start my own coup?"

Philip threw his hands in the air. "Not one noble has come forward to accuse you. Can I trust no one? Whose side would they be on, if not mine? At this rate, I'll have to look outside the kingdom to find Anna a husband!"

"Don't be so dramatic." Torgon moved his queen to take the pawn, leaving his knight undefended. "I believe them all to be trustworthy and utterly loyal. Many of them would make fine matches for your sister. Lord Arrys's nephew is a good man, and the one I think would be best."

"But how did he react when you approached him with plans to overthrow me?"

Torgon sighed watching Philip remove the defeated knight from the board. "He told me never to speak of it again."

"What does that mean exactly?"

"I think it means that he won't entertain such talk."

"Or it could mean that he's seeing to the plans himself."

Torgon shook his head. "I think you're being paranoid again."

"How are we supposed to know the difference?" Philip asked, falling back into his armchair.

"I believe they're giving me the benefit of the doubt and a chance to be loyal." Torgon continued hovering over the board. "If I made a bad choice, wouldn't you chastise me first then give me the chance to atone for my mistake?"

Philip sipped his wine before answering, "I don't have that luxury. Those in my rule must be punished according to their crime. I can't afford to grant second chances."

"But you do." Torgon shifted his eyes to Philip, but retained the same concentration. "With a just mind and heart, you grant second chances more than you realize. I believe these men are attempting to emulate the king they love." Looking back down at the board, he said, "You've been in check for three moves."

———

Hiro arrived in Kingstor Noble from behind the mountains overlooking the great city. With mountains to the north and west of King's Forest, Teardrop Sea to the east, and Crying River cutting across the south, Kingstor Noble was almost impenetrable—at least by land. Hiro crawled over the mountains until he met the gushing waterfall at the edge of King's Forest. The large forest to the west of Kingstor was the only undefended section, thus a wall had been built dividing the king's magnificent forest and the common homes and farms on the other side. Had a human tried to cross the wall where it met the mountains, they would have been washed away by dangerous, rushing waterfalls. Even in winter, when the water froze, the falls were nearly impossible to scale—unless you had claws.

Hiro didn't wait atop the falls. Instead he hid under some trees that had somehow grown into a cave-like form. Their trunks weaved a flawless roof with just enough room for a dragon to crawl inside. As the sun slipped beyond the horizon, the black dragon watched between the soft green growth along the branches.

Many glowing creatures appeared in springtime. Nocturnal snorks began wriggling up the sides of the tree trunks, not bothering with a dragon nearby, knowing they would cause fatal effects if they were eaten. The miniscule glow of puffertongs drifted through the air toward the powerful falls. Even the forest floor brightened with old snork slime that was disturbed when the hooves of Anna's horse trotted over it toward Hiro's hiding place.

She dismounted, but didn't bother to tie her horse. When she pushed her heavy cloak aside, Hiro could see she had thick boots on her feet, leather gloves on her hands, and a bag full of supplies over one shoulder. She turned her back to Hiro and started toward the falls.

Without warning Hiro burst from the trees and covered the ground between them in a few strides. Before Anna could turn, Hiro grabbed her around the waist with one claw and sprang into the trees. She gave a startled squeak and he bumbled her slightly in his grasp. With a few springs up the steep mountainside, he came to rest at the top of the waterfall's edge.

"What was the meaning of that?" Anna barked when Hiro sat her on a rock at the water's edge.

"I needed a memory of your capture for Rakgar," Hiro said with only a small grin on his lips. "I thought it would look better if I surprised you."

She rolled her eyes at him then looked out over the vista. "Where do we go now?"

"Back to the Rock Clouds."

The woman spun to face him again. "The Rock Clouds? Is that necessary?"

"Unfortunately, yes," Hiro said. "I tried to talk him out of it, but Rakgar insisted I bring you back."

"But your laws!" Anna's hands flew to her throat. "If he talks to me!"

Hiro shook his head. "Rakgar has decreed you exempt from the Killing Law. It is officially lawful for me to speak to you…this time."

Her look of confusion gave way to relief before growing into concern. "What will he do with me?" she whispered.

"You won't be harmed."

She shook her head in disbelief. "A single human among dragons? I'll never return, will I?"

"You will." Hiro's heart began to harden at the sorrow on her face. "I give you my wyrd that no dragon will lift a claw against you and you'll be returned unmolested."

"Your wyrd?"

"My wyrd, Anna." He offered her his open claw. "May you strike me down if I break it."

5

OUST

"Sire! I demand a private audience!"

Philip barely had time to be startled at his office door banging open with this announcement before people began spilling through it. Two guards followed a nobleman and his servant; one of the guards stumbled and caught himself from falling as he attempted to reach the nobleman. General Torgon stepped through last, unimpeded and calm.

"My apologies, Sire." The staff guard who remained on his feet attempted to step in front of the nobleman. "I explained that I would announce his Lordship, but he wouldn't wait."

The nobleman's servant had been clamoring to keep the second guard's hands from his master, but failed. "It's all right." Philip raised a hand to calm the guards in their pursuit to extricate the man. "I'll see him."

The nobleman jerked his arm free of the guard, but didn't face the king. He lifted one finger to point at the door. "Out," he hissed. The man eyed everyone, even his own servant, until they all left. When only Torgon remained, the nobleman repeated the demand, directing it at the Royal General.

Torgon tilted his head toward Philip. "I'm sorry," Philip said, rising from his chair, "but only the king has the right to order the Royal General."

The nobleman spun on his heel. Getting a good look at the man did nothing to improve Philip's first impression. Small, close-set eyes hunkered under bushy eyebrows. The man's high cheekbones might have made others consider him good-looking in his earlier years, but his slack jowls and the gray hair above his ears now emphasized his age. Philip couldn't tell if the man's lips were naturally thin, or pursed in anger.

"Sire," the man dipped his head, "with all due respect, General Torgon is the subject of my interruption."

Torgon nodded behind the man.

"Then," Philip resumed his seat behind his desk, "it makes even more sense for him to stay."

The man's lips disappeared into his mouth altogether. He glanced at Torgon, who kept a stony face, and settled his gilded half-cloak behind him as he took a seat without it being offered.

"You'll have to remind me of your name, sir." Philip pushed aside the reports he had been reading. Looking up, he noticed the man had sat on the edge of his chair, back straight and hands on thighs. Every tooth the nobleman.

"Lord Dieko of Selevyn, Your Majesty. I have yet to overtake my father's, Lord Diedric's, estate in Selevyn. But I have been to court several times this past year. I was in attendance when the faeries first came to Kingstor Noble in the winter and I attended Your Majesty's coronation."

None of these details mattered, of course. Any noble who could prove their rights could attend court and even the coronation; although Dieko must have supplanted himself in another Kingstor noble's home to have remained in the city this long. Selevyn was two counties over and several days away as the dragon flies.

Before Philip could ask more, Dieko continued. "I swore fealty to Your Majesty as a representative of the House of Selevyn only months ago. And I've come to uphold that oath." He glanced at Torgon.

Torgon leaned against the wall. He didn't blink.

Dieko pressed his lips together again before turning back to Philip. "I'm afraid I bear ill tidings of your Royal General's loyalties, Sire."

Philip leaned on one arm of his chair. His face remained a smooth mask. "Is that so?"

"Yes, Sire." Dieko's chin fell to his chest and didn't rise. "I'm afraid Royal General Torgon has been…" Dieko glanced back up at Torgon before lifting his nose into the air. "I accuse Royal General Torgon Ido Bragon of treason and conspiracy."

Philip blinked. "Go on."

Dieko's lips disappeared again. "General Torgon has been attempting to conspire to usurp the throne of the Noble Kingdom, Sire." He pointed a finger at the general.

"He told me he wanted to see someone else on the throne. He called you a 'young know-nothing' and said the kingdom would be better off without you on the throne."

Philip swayed his head toward Torgon. "'Young know-nothing'?"

Torgon shrugged.

Philip turned back to Dieko. "You heard him say this?"

If it was possible, Dieko sat up straighter. "I did, Sire. I'm sorry to bring to light such a horrible betrayal."

Philip scrunched up his face. "'Young know-nothing'?"

"Don't mock me," Torgon finally spoke as he stepped to Philip's side. "You try to do better."

Dieko's lips finally materialized as the bottom one hung open. His eyes bulged as his finger lifted. "You knew?" he mumbled.

Grins spread across both the king's and his general's faces. "I'm sorry," Philip said, "Lord Dieko, you've fallen victim to a rather unorthodox attempt to find loyalty among the gentlemen of my court." He rose from his chair to circle out in front of the lord. "The good news is two-fold. Well, three-fold if you count Torgon's innocence." He nodded to his general for good measure.

Settling on the edge of the front of his desk, Philip held his hands out to Dieko. "Not only have you proven yourself to be of unfailing loyalty to your king, you've also won the hand of my sister."

"Your sister?" Dieko took a breath, but then finally composed himself enough to close his mouth.

"I still don't agree with your method, Philip." Torgon started through the door to his office, but ducked back again to add, "Oh, congratulations on the coming nuptials, Dieko. I wish you and Anna all the best."

"Anna?" Dieko's low eyebrows reversed their drooping course on his forehead. "Anna?" he asked Philip.

"Yes, Anna, my sister." Philip nodded and walked back to his chair. "We'll make the announcement after I inform her. I'm sure she'll want to meet you as soon as possible. Why don't you plan to come to dinner? We can tell her then."

"Dinner? Oh, yes, Sire," Dieko nodded and stood. Stepping toward the door, he swung it open, but stopped to turn back again. "Thank you, Sire."

———

"Hiro!" Anna called from his claw, "I'm sorry, but I can't make it much longer."

Hiro snaked his neck down to look at her without altering his course. "What's wrong?"

The woman's eyes sagged and her one arm around his claw was doing little to hold her in place. "I'm tired. I need to sleep."

"We've only been flying a few hours," he grumbled back.

"I'm sorry, I've been riding all day and I can't seem to—" her voice faltered and her legs slipped in his claw before she could right herself.

Hiro tilted a wing toward the ground. Circling in the dark, he couldn't see any openings in the trees. He couldn't see anything in the trees. He might land amidst banshees or lions or worse, but he dove into them anyway.

Anna lolled in his claw once he landed. She didn't make any noise, so he was able to hear the thumping of several large hearts nearby. "We can't stop here," he whispered to her.

SNARF! Her own snort wasn't enough to wake her. Anna's eyes were closed and her mouth hung open.

"Wake up, woman!" he whispered harshly as he threw her onto his back.

"What—ouch!"

"Quiet!" he whispered as loud as he dared.

Once she latched on around his neck, Hiro ran. He hurtled through the trees with barely a sound.

"What is it?" Anna whispered into the dark.

"I'm not sure." Hiro didn't slow. "It sounded like large hearts beating. As big as scorrands or paquars, nothing smaller. Many of them. Perhaps more than a dozen."

"But scorrands and paquars wouldn't harm us unless they were provoked."

"And it could have been something else altogether."

Hiro's claws clacked against rock, echoing in the night. He slid to a halt when a great stone wall barred his way.

"What is it?" Anna whispered again against his scales.

"I don't know." Hiro tip-taloned next to the wall. Leaves and branches covered an opening at the side. He pulled the vegetation away and stepped through.

He closed his eyes to listen. All he could hear were a few snakes and small lizards. Some birds roosting atop the walls. Insects in the crevices of the stones. No larger animals nearby.

Opening his eyes, he saw the wall they had come through wrapped around to complete the outer walls of an abandoned building. A few trees grew inside the structure, extending above the missing roof. Anna sat up, wonder evident in her voice. "Did someone dare live in the Black Forest?"

"You're lucky they did." Hiro reached up to pull her from his back. "There's nothing harmful nearby. We'll sleep here."

He set her out of the way, then burned a large circle in the overgrown floor. Settling down on the warm scorch marks, Hiro realized his own lethargy from the day's journey. He lifted a wing and a claw and Anna scuttled under them.

6

TERRIBLE HABITS

"What do you mean, she can't be found?" Philip struggled to keep his voice steady.

The guard knelt to the side of the dining table, but didn't lift his head to answer the king. Lord Dieko sat to Philip's right and Torgon sat on his left. The starter meal had been served while they waited for word of Anna's whereabouts, but the mid-meal was long overdue now.

"Did you search her chambers?" Philip asked. "The gardens? The library? The map rooms? The Hall of Kings?"

"The forest?" Torgon muttered.

"Did you question her maid?" Philip continued, brushing past the comment.

"Yes, Majesty." The guard lifted his head only to lower it again. "She claims the princess departed into the forest on a ride, but hasn't returned to her chambers yet. We'll continue our search."

He stood to leave, but Philip called again. "Wait, General Torgon is right." Philip nodded to himself. "Get a party together and search the forest. If she's gone out to the mountains again, she needs to learn she can't do that any longer."

Once the guard left, Torgon cleared his throat. "It was only a toothy comment. She hasn't disappeared like this for weeks."

"No," Philip waved to Ruther—filling in tonight for his brother Murthur as the king's personal servant—to bring the food. "You're right. If she has disappeared, she needs to be taught a lesson. If something has happened to her, we need to find her. Either way, a search party is warranted."

"Sire?" Philip tried to not to jerk his head when Dieko spoke. He had entirely forgotten the man was there. "Does the princess really disappear often? I've heard others speak of her wandering, but one can never be sure of the difference between truth and rumor."

Philip tried to hold himself back from digging in as the aromatic, hot food was placed in front of him. "She did have a tendency to disappear when she first came to the Noble Kingdom, but she was improving lately, as Torgon said. I believed she had changed."

Philip lifted a bite of succulent meat to his mouth, but stopped when Dieko said, "Changed from what, Sire?"

Philip put the bite back on his plate with a sigh only partially meant for the man at his right. "Dieko, you'll be promised to Anna soon enough, so I can be honest with you, correct?"

"Of course, Sire."

Philip took a deep breath. "Dieko, Anna was raised in the mountains, as everyone knows. Yes, she was trained as a noble during that time. But what the kingdom doesn't know is that Anna has a bad habit of disappearing. Often.

"She actually disappeared for a couple of weeks in the fall and came back looking like the bottom of a rotting log. She had a lantern with dragon fire in it and wild promises that no dragon was threatening the kingdom." Philip shook his head and picked up his fork again. "I don't know what to make of her behavior anymore," he added before finally putting the bite into his mouth.

Dieko lifted his own fork. "Perhaps marriage will temper her, Sire."

———

"Again?!"

"I'm sorry, but I'm accustomed to certain things!" Hiro roared, not caring who heard him.

"You don't have to be that way about it!" Anna called up at him. "It will only be for a moment."

He landed harder than he had yet. "What is it this time?"

"None of your business." She hopped out of his claw, but stopped to look at the dragon before moving off. "Did you check for danger?"

He pressed his nose to within a claw length from hers. "I'm the danger to you, woman. Now what do you need to stop for this time?"

"It's private." She moved toward some trees.

"Oh no you don't!" He slithered between her and the trees. "You need to stop and eat. You need to stop and rest. You need to stretch your pretty legs. You need to gather water. You need to get rocks out of your boots. You need to stop DELAYING!" he roared. "Tell me what it is this time or I won't stop again!"

"If you must know," she side-stepped to wriggle around him, "it's a human bodily function. You wouldn't understand."

He wrapped his tail around her waist and put her back in front of him. "Try me."

She dropped her bag and punched her fists onto her hips. "It's not a pleasant subject for either you or me, dragon."

"You've seen me cry!"

She rolled her eyes. Throwing her hands in the air, she groaned. "Fine! You want to know. I'll tell you." She tapped her foot and ground her teeth some more. "I have to…I need to…well…chinkle."

"Chinkle?" Hiro's top lip pulled back. "What's that?"

Anna groaned again. "I don't have time to explain!" She pushed past his claws and dashed toward the trees.

"Then I'll watch."

She whirled on him with wide eyes. "I beg your pardon!"

Hiro wanted to grin at how big her eyes grew, but settled on a smirk. "Perhaps I'll understand better if I see it."

"You'll do nothing of the sort!" she barked.

"You've seen me CRY!"

"I don't care if I watched you make an egg! You're not coming into those trees with me!"

"Are you trying to escape?"

"Have you lost your mind?!"

Hiro shrugged a shoulder. "This could be a ploy to try anything."

"How dare you!" She shifted on her feet. "I came with you willingly! I'm trusting you! How can you…?" She shifted again and looked at the trees. "Fine. Watch if you must!"

Hiro followed her into the trees.

Moments later the dragon bolted from the trees. "That's disgusting!!" he roared. "How on this green world can you do something like that?!" He clawed at the ground. "Disgusting! Disgusting!"

Anna stepped from the trees, adjusting her skirts. "I told you not to watch."

"Ugh!" Hiro grumbled, "humans are disgusting!"

"You're disgusting for insisting on watching," she snapped at him.

Hiro waved his head back and forth. "But it's a waste product, correct? That means it's filth!"

"Yes," Anna said, punching her little fists on her hips, "it's a waste product, but that doesn't mean it's as disgusting as all that."

"Would you eat it?" he asked. "Save it? Use it for something?"

"Sometimes the more solid waste can be used to fertilize the ground to grow plants."

"Plants that you eat?"

Anna pinched her face to the side. "Actually, it can only be used for non-edible plants, but it still—"

"So, there are toxins unsuitable for consumption!"

"Yes, but—"

"Filth!" he barked. "And useless filth at that!"

"It's just a byproduct!" Anna threw her hands in the air. "Even dragons have that!"

"Good clean fire! And I understand the mechanics, but that doesn't make it any less disgusting!"

Anna pointed back into the trees. "That was mostly water anyway!"

"Water?" Hiro hesitated. "Wait!" He sat up straight. "You never stopped to do that when we were traveling together in the fall."

"Oh, uh," Anna became very interested in adjusting her bag over her shoulder. "Well, I, er, knew how dire the situation was...I thought, um, we shouldn't stop often...No one would know if I..." her voice trailed off in a whisper.

Hiro bent to meet her eye as she inspected the forest floor. "What did you do?"

"Well..." she hemmed again, "you see, I didn't think anyone would notice because everything on and...around me was...already wet..."

Hiro's eyes drifted to his front claw. "AAACKKK!" he screamed very undragon-like, "you chinkled in my claw!"

"Now, really," Anna put her hands on her hips again, "you never would've known—"

"AAACCCKKKK!!" Hiro coughed up a fireball and spit it onto his claw.

"Is that really necessary—"

Hiro's eyes bulged at her as he scratched one claw against the other. "Necessary? Necessary?! I've a mind to go to Kradik and have him cut it off!!"

"Don't you think you're over—"

"I can't get it off!" Hiro rolled on the ground spitting fire on his claw and arm while scratching at it. "I can't get it off!!"

Anna crossed her arms at her chest. "If you're quite done, I can't ride in your claw with it in that state."

7

GAMES

Out of courtesy Philip and Torgon included Dieko in their ritual of chess after dinner. Not feeling entirely comfortable with Dieko, Philip passed on a match with Torgon and let Dieko test himself. Dieko claimed only a minor ability with the game, but Philip watched Torgon grit his teeth against the elder nobleman. Torgon won the first round, but Dieko won the second. As they began a third game, a knock came at the door.

A messenger entered, but hung his head while standing in the entryway to catch his breath. "Dire news, Your Majesty." The man's eyes flickered to Dieko.

"Speak freely, man," Philip prompted. "What's happened?"

He wrung his hands, staring at the floor. "The princess's horse returned alone, Sire. Just after the search party mounted. They traced its path all the way to the edge of the King's Forest, to the waterfall at the end of the wall." He continued working his jaw, but nothing more came out.

Dieko stood. "Out with it, man," he hissed low, but the words couldn't be mistaken for anything other than a command.

The messenger looked up at Dieko, unblinking. "There were claw marks," he shifted his eyes to the king, "as big as the horse itself. They were within breathing distance of the horse's hoofprints. The guards are certain. They continue to search for any trace of the princess, but sent word back with me." The man bowed his head again. "A dragon has taken the princess."

———

"Did you ever chinkle on my back?"

"No."

"Did you ever chinkle while you slept next to me?"

"No."

"Did you ever chinkle on Tog?"

"No."

"Only on me?"

"You're special."

"You're disgusting."

Hiro and Anna trudged together through the trees of the Black Forest. He couldn't bring himself to pick her up again. Anna jumped over a large root. "I've heard that some animals chinkle on things to mark them as their own." She shifted her eyes under long eyelashes to Hiro. "Does that make you mine?"

He put his nose in front of her and snorted, blowing her hair out behind her. "Dragons can't be owned."

"But you claim when a dame accepts a dan's heart that she can control him," she said with a smile. "So at least a dan can be owned. Else what do you call it?"

"We call it love. What do humans call it?"

"If it's a female marrying…" Her voice trailed off.

"Yes?" he asked, suspecting he had hit on a sore spot.

"Never mind." She bit off the words and kept walking.

Hiro ran to catch up with a smile on his lips, but stopped when a breeze met him. "Stop!" he ordered her.

"Stop what?" she asked, turning.

Hiro lifted his head, turning his nose into the wind. "I smell," he inhaled deeply, then quickly shifted his eyes to meet hers, "other dragons."

"Here?" Anna searched the trees. "Have they come for me?"

Hiro shook his head. "No, the scent…it's not…right…"

Anna trailed after him as he followed the scent through the trees. "What do you mean, 'not right'?"

"I mean, there's something wrong with it." Ignoring her protests and warnings, Hiro crawled through the enormous trees toward the scent. The Black Forest spared little light from above when no leaves were on the trees, but with new growth on them, it might as well have been dusk.

The scent of dragons grew stronger as Hiro crept along, sweeping his nose from side to side. He didn't recognize the scents from anyone he knew, but he could smell the bitter tang of the Rock Clouds. Whoever had been here had come from his home. But the smell of fire—the burnt, scorched, flavor of heat—smelled too strong.

"It's almost as if—" Then he saw them.

"As if what?" Anna asked, pushing past his tail.

Hiro threw a claw out to stop her from moving forward. "Don't touch them."

"Don't touch what?"

Hiro put his claw back down and stepped forward. Pointing, he showed her where light gray spots covered the ground in several places among the trees.

Anna bent over to inspect one such spot. "Ashes."

Hiro sniffed the remains. "None of them are from the same dragon," he told her.

"But the piles," she stood up straighter, "they're so small."

Hiro pointed out marks against the ground where the dirt had been displaced. He couldn't bring himself to speak.

"Boot prints," Anna whispered. "Humans did this."

Hiro growled looking at several sets of the boot prints dancing around the scant remains. "Rakgar was right. Humans aren't afraid of dragons any longer. They hunt us for sport and—"

"—gather the ashes," Anna finished. When Hiro crawled next to her, she pointed to the evidence. "They made a campfire here. Probably to wait until the ashes were cool enough to transport. I can see wagon marks here and here." She pointed out the different tracks. "This was no accident. It was planned."

"How?" Hiro rumbled in his throat. "How did they do this? I see no burnt or broken trees as would accompany a fight."

Scanning the area again, Anna nodded. "You're right. There's nothing but the ash marks."

"No," Hiro whispered, glaring at the gray patches. "No, no, no." He ran around the spots on the ground and skidded to a halt in front of Anna. "They're in a circle."

Anna's brow furrowed. "What does it mean?"

Hiro hung his head. "They were sleeping."

"That's not sport," Anna said, shaking her own head in disbelief.

"It's slaughter." Hiro growled at the marks on the ground. He paced closer to one of the thin piles.

"Wait," Anna's head continued shaking, "how is this even possible? Even with men surrounding them on all sides and taking shots with dragon-killer bolts, none of them would have died instantly. The bolts are powerful, but you've been struck by them and survived. The dames would have woken and fought."

"Does a massacre need to make sense?" Hiro reached out to the pile in front of him. The scent was vaguely familiar. He must have at least met this dame before. He scooped a small pile of ash into his claw, trying desperately to remember what she looked like, and he hung his head. Someone needed to mourn her.

Pulling his claw away, he uncovered the point of an arrowhead in the dirt. His top lip curled back on its own as he let the ash fall to the ground again and he picked up the tiny piece of metal.

"Hiro!" Anna called from the other side of the circle. She waved him over to show him another arrow embedded in the dirt.

"I found one too." He showed her the arrowhead in his claw. "They didn't even use bolts."

Anna picked up the arrow, turning it over in her hand. "Arrows couldn't do this. We know that from experience."

"They were killed while sleeping before they could fight back, Anna." Hiro hung his head again. "May their embers burn forever."

"Hiro, you don't understand," Anna stepped closer to him with the arrow in her hand. "My brother is planning something. He's been locked up in private counsel with the faeries ever since I returned the last time."

"Do you have any idea what those plans might be?"

She shook her head. "No, he claims that the faeries insisted I not be included in the plans."

"And he doesn't trust you enough to tell you anyway." It wasn't really a question. Hiro knew that Philip didn't trust Anna.

"He doesn't know me well enough to trust me," Anna said as she hung her head and fiddled with the arrow.

"I couldn't say," Hiro answered, then surveyed the remains again. "I *can* say that dragons are stronger than this."

Anna rubbed the arrowhead with her thumb. Her eyes creased with worry, then narrowed as she scrubbed at it harder. "There's something on this," she muttered. She reached into her bag and pulled out a water skin similar to the one she had made from a lydik stomach the last time she and Hiro were together. She trickled water over the arrow point and rubbed away the ashes. Splashing more water down the length of the arrow revealed that the arrow point was covered in a black substance.

Anna continued to rub at it without the water. "It looks like a paint or lacquer of some sort." Her head jerked up to meet Hiro's eyes. "A poison maybe? But I can't think of a poison that would leave behind a black residue like this. Can you? Hiro, can you think of anything that would harm a dragon like this?"

Hiro surveyed the remains, but his mind flickered to the flarote bulb. If dragons ate too much of it, it would kill them. But these dragons weren't force-fed. He shook his head at Anna. "Dragons don't have weaknesses."

———

They decided to get some rest alongside the piles of ashes then fly the remainder of the way to the Rock Clouds in one trip. Curled up on the opposite side of where the humans had camped, Hiro could still pick up their scent.

He snorted, turning his head away from the stench. "Do you think the humans that killed the dames ever chinkled in this area?"

Anna nuzzled under Hiro's front leg. "Most likely."

"Humans are disgusting."

"You've told me that you sometimes vomit fire," Anna replied with a hint of annoyance. "Wouldn't you consider that disgusting as well?"

"Of course not," Hiro shrugged. "It's fire. It devours, not desecrates."

"Humans vomit too."

"More of that nasty stuff from your insides?"

Anna sighed. "Yes."

"Disgusting."

Anna's breathing slowed. Hiro could feel her chest rising higher with her inhalation and he thought she had fallen asleep. She surprised him when she spoke, and her voice caught. "What will Rakgar do to me when we arrive?"

His claws instinctively closed around her a little more. "He won't harm you. I give you my wyrd." He forced himself to relax his claws. Why would he promise her that? What unnatural hold did this woman have upon him?

"Hiro," she whispered again. "You understand that I would never condone this sort of action toward dragons, don't you? You know, if I could, I would do everything in my power to stop it." When he didn't answer immediately, she fussed in his claws until she could stare him in the eye. "You know that, don't you?"

His burning heart, deep in his chest, contracted for a moment. He dipped his chin to her. "Yes, Anna. I know."

8

INCEPTION

"You can swallow me, but I can swallow you."

Anna squirmed in Hiro's claw. "You're making them much harder now, aren't you?"

"It wouldn't be fun if it was easy," he rumbled.

Anna sighed and fidgeted some more. Finally she shouted, "Water!"

Hiro's smile faded, but it didn't disappear.

"Always old, sometimes new. Never sad, sometimes blue. Never empty, sometimes full. Never pushes, always pulls."

Hiro's smile disappeared. "Say it again."

Anna repeated the riddle as the pair drew closer to the Rock Clouds. The sun was just dipping over the horizon, turning the sky a soft purple and pink. The three moons of Avonoa shined their half-moon light on the tip of the towering Inner Mountain. Several glittering shapes flew into the air in the distance, but none approached them. Yet.

He asked Anna to repeat the riddle again. As he thought about it, Hiro noticed two large, dark shapes detach themselves from the bottom of the closest floating mountain. This particular mountain was so large and moved so slowly that the two dragons could have been attached to it all day. The moons glittered off their scales and Hiro hissed.

"The moons," he said to Anna, keeping his voice low, "but you forgot the last line. 'What are we?' That's why I couldn't guess it."

Anna shrugged. "That makes it too easy. It's your turn."

"Quiet," he whispered down to her. "They're coming."

Anna folded herself over in his claw. Hiro tightened his grip around her waist and legs. They had abandoned her bag of supplies earlier near Centaur River when she insisted on making one last disgusting stop. She couldn't look "too prepared," as Hiro had put it. They even discussed how she must look as if she had come with him against her will.

"Don't speak unless you are spoken to," Hiro whispered again. "I'll do all I can to keep you safe. You have my wyrd."

Anna leaned over away from the wind as if she'd been hanging there for the entire flight. "I know you will," she whispered back.

After several wingfalls, the two approaching dragons announced themselves with a roar. Hiro noticed the orange-tinged brown of Trakillyn's wings, but didn't recognize the other dragon. The pair hovered in front of Hiro while they searched the form of the slumped princess, then they swung to opposite sides of him to escort Hiro and his cargo back to the Rock Clouds.

In silence, they flew past The Watch perches under the slow-moving mountain. In his peripheral vision Hiro saw no fewer than five triangular heads shift in their direction. As the small group skirted the mountains and floating boulders, Hiro could hear wings take to the skies behind them. Rocks clattered as more dragons followed. Even the groan of the floating mountains eased in awe as the first human ever known to have entered the Rock Clouds arrived.

Trakillyn and his companion landed to the sides of Rakgar's lair. Hiro halted in front of the opening, but hesitated before entering. He turned to Trakillyn, his jaw opening slightly to question the brown dragon, when he saw Tog crawl up behind him. When Hiro met his best friend's eye, Tog shook his head ever so slightly.

Instead of speaking, Hiro dumped Anna onto the rocks in front of the lair. Her entire body shook as she blundered to her feet. Trying to soften his heart against her, Hiro shoved her toward the lair. She caught herself with a yelp, then crawled away from the dragons sitting outside and went through the dark entrance.

Hiro followed her, nudging her forward all the way. When they reached the dimming light of the cave beyond, Anna blinked into the dark settling around them.

"Hiro," Rakgar purred. Hiro could sense a touch of a grin in that voice.

As if by signal, several lights glowed in the darkness. Milah and Mitashio spat large rocks out of their mouths, the heat burning them white hot. The faerie Skorkot whispered some words into her hand and unfurled a shimmering ribbon that she wrapped around her wrist. Three more dragons in the back spat fire on a large log.

Rakgar stepped forward into the circle of light created. "I see you were successful in your assignment," he growled, circling the woman. Her breath quickened, but she managed to put on a fairly convincing shocked face at his spoken words.

Hiro leaned toward the massive gray dragon and breathed the memory of Princess Anna with her back toward him at the waterfall. He concentrated on only sending the memory of snatching her from the trees and leaping into the air.

When Rakgar blinked the memory away, Hiro spoke. "I easily took her as she wandered about in the forest."

Rakgar gazed at Hiro while he breathed the memory into Milah's face, who in turn passed it to the others. After much too long for Hiro's comfort, Rakgar nodded and turned to Anna. "And you, woman, do you know why you're here?"

Anna pulled her cloak tighter around her. "No," she whispered, staring at the dragons around her with feigned surprise.

Rakgar bared his fangs at her. "Your brother, King Philip, is attacking dragons. He sets traps. He kills in great numbers." Rakgar leveled his head at her. "Does he not fear us?"

"If you can speak, perhaps you should discuss it with him," Anna said, allowing her expression to rest. "If he knew you are intelligent creatures, I'm sure he wouldn't behave in such a manner."

Rakgar rumbled in his throat. "Humans are the monsters. Why do you think we hide from you the fact that we can speak?"

Anna's head dipped. "If you've brought me here to convince me of your power it won't help. My brother doesn't keep my counsel."

"And if he did?"

Anna gazed up at the enormous dragon. She barely came up to his leg joint, but Hiro could swear he saw anger and defiance in her eyes. "You would have nothing to fear."

Rakgar gave a guttered, hesitating roar. Hiro recognized the familiar chuckle he hadn't heard for several months. When Rakgar brought his head back to the woman in front of him, he snapped his jaws at her, but Hiro could still see the smile on his lips. "We *have* nothing to fear."

"Then why have you brought me here?" she asked.

"To remind your brother and all humans how dangerous a dragon can be."

Anna glanced around the cave while Rakgar stepped away to join the other dragons surrounding her. "Will you return me, then?" she asked his retreating back. Hiro had never heard her sound so meek.

Rakgar glared at Hiro. "Perhaps."

"Rakgar," Hiro spoke, attempting to soften his heart again, "let every being know I've given this woman my wyrd that she wouldn't be harmed. If anything happens to her, they have broken my wyrd in my stead and their life is mine."

Rakgar lifted his top lip to reveal his fangs at Hiro. "Why would you do that?"

"You know she needs to go back," Hiro insisted. "Unharmed."

Snorting flame from his nostrils, Rakgar turned to Anna. He pointed one claw toward the small opening leading to Priya's lair. "Then you will stay as my guest. Go in there and a green dragon will attend you."

"Priya?" Hiro's head jolted up. "Has Priya returned?"

Rakgar watched Anna step toward the opening before swiveling his head to Hiro. "She has."

"Where has she been?" Hiro stepped toward the same opening. "What happened? I must see her!"

But Rakgar moved to block his way. "I will send her to you after she's done with the woman."

Hiro watched Anna go. Before she went through the dark entrance, she glanced back at Hiro. She gave him a reassuring smile and a nod, then slipped into the darkness beyond.

"Rakgar," Hiro said after Anna disappeared, "along the way here, I saw something…" He shook his head.

Rakgar's brows creased. "What is it, Hiro?"

"Ashes," he whispered, "so many ashes." He placed his nose in front of Rakgar's and sent him the memory of the piles of ashes. He sent only the sight of it, as well as the sight of the arrow in his claw.

Rakgar's frown deepened as he gave the memory to Milah. Turning back to Hiro, Rakgar said, "We know the humans have been attacking dragons."

"But they were killed in their sleep. Instantly. There was no sign of struggle." Hiro's scales lifted in anger. "What human can even do that? I would also like to find out why Philip is gathering dragon ash."

Rakgar nodded in thought. "Yes," he answered, "you should go back to investigate. I'll send Priya to your lair and the two of you must go to the surface immediately. Discover what you can, then return."

Hiro nodded, but hesitated before leaving. His eyes flickered toward the entrance to Priya's lair. Rakgar noticed the movement. "Don't worry, Hiro. I'll send her to you straight away."

9

VALIDATIONS

"An entire quiver?" Philip asked the lieutenant standing in front of him. "Where is it?"

The man had presented himself in the audience hall as one of the company that had traveled north with Captain Murzod and the faeries. He was not a young man, as evidenced by the gray at his temples. But given his petite frame—he was smaller than some of the maids in the palace—Philip could imagine he'd be the swiftest on a horse. He had introduced himself as Jakobi.

Pushing aside his riding cloak, Jakobi revealed a small satchel hanging from one shoulder. "They've enchanted it, Sire," he said, loosening the buckle. "If I may. The halfway point I've come from will be used to distribute many more like these." He pulled an entire quiver from the small bag, something Philip knew would be impossible without majik. Jakobi handed the quiver to Philip with a small bow.

The quiver was nondescript leather, but black fletching with gilt on the edges poked out of the top. Philip pulled one free to inspect the tip. His stomach clenched when he saw the blackened arrowhead tip. An uneven smattered line circled the shaft showing where it had been dipped into the deadly substance.

Philip and Torgon shared a glance before he slid the arrow back into the quiver. "Are there any more?" Philip asked Jakobi.

The lieutenant shook his head. "I'm afraid not, Sire. The rest of the small supply made has been sent to groups of soldiers setting traps for more ash."

Philip struggled not to grind his teeth. "Under whose authority?"

Jakobi hesitated, "Captain Murzod and the faeries, of course, Sire. He distributed the arrows to the men then sent me to give you the quiver and this." He handed Philip a rolled scroll of parchment sealed with Murzod's house seal.

Philip broke it and swiftly read the messy handwriting. When he finished he thrust it at Torgon. "Days late in his report and he presumes to anticipate my orders. They've done nothing more than set up a halfway point and they barely reached The Great Northern Mountain alive."

"I suppose we could be pleased that he's only days behind instead of weeks," Torgon answered with a frown.

"I suppose we should be pleased he's behind at all," Philip muttered to the floor. Remembering the lieutenant, he forced his attention back to the man. "I'm sorry Jakobi, you must be tired. If that's all of your report, you should get some rest tonight and report back to General Tommak in the morning. You'll have to guide the next convoy with dragon ash back to Captain Murzod."

But Jakobi didn't turn to leave. "Actually, Sire, there is something else I think I should mention." His head dipped, but his eyes reconnected to Philip's. "My report from Captain Murzod is complete, but I came upon a slaughtered group of staff soldiers on my way to Kingstor. There were five bodies. They had bags and shovels. The bodies were lain out on the ground with the shovels on their chests and the bags over their heads." He dropped his eyes. "They were surrounding a pile of dragon ash and there were centaur hoofprints everywhere. I believe the centaurs came upon the men gathering the ash and killed them for it. They laid the bodies out that way to send a message."

Philip exhaled slowly. "I've been taught that centaurs believe dragon ash to be sacred." He nodded before turning to Torgon. "Add a caution to the proclamation for gold in exchange for dragon ash. Let the people know they need to avoid centaurs above all else." Nodding to Jakobi, he added, "It's not worth getting killed."

———

Hiro paced across the hard floor of his lair. In one corner, he had added a few pine boughs to sleep on. Since his stay in Jarek's barn in the fall, he felt much more comfortable lying down with something to soften the rock beneath him. But it did nothing to distract him from the conversation of the moment.

"What if we hurt her just a little?" Prak offered. "It might scare her enough to convince the king to leave dragons alone."

Hiro spun around in time to see Tog's eye roll. "If we hurt her at all, the king himself would climb up here and rip out our throats," Tog told the smaller dragon. "That's the problem."

"We shouldn't have her here at all," Hiro growled. "I don't know what Rakgar is thinking making me bring her here."

"And allowing her to hear us speak?" Prak echoed their thoughts. "Even if most humans think she's gone mad from the experience, there will likely be those who believe her. That's how ideas start, with a flicker of the truth. I mean, even some dragons think we should speak to the humans, right?" At Tog's shocked eyes, he quickly added, "I'm not saying that's what I think, but there's got to be some semblance of truth in there somewhere. Humans may not be able to handle it right now, but they may be in the future. Maybe they could get used to the idea. Maybe they—"

"Blasphemy!" Tog roared.

"I know, I know," Prak continued unabashedly, "I'm just saying that's what some dragons think."

"Not all dragons can be trusted with secrets," a smooth voice came from the entrance. The three dragons spun to see Priya sidle through the entrance. "As is evidenced by The Krusible."

"Priya!" Prak bounced to his feet. "Where've you been? Were you on the surface? You know, some others said you've been here all this time hiding in your lair. Were you having adventures? Did you visit the desert ruck? Did you visit the island ruck? They're much further away; I can imagine it would take a long time to get there and back. You were gone so long!"

"No, Prak," she said before he could continue his questions. But she offered no explanation. Turning to Hiro she said, "I believe you and I have an assignment to complete."

"Can I come too?" The inevitable question came from the small brown dragon.

"No, Prak," Priya repeated, again with no explanation, although she kept her eyes on Hiro.

"Come on, Prak," Tog heaved himself from the ground. "I hear Likkop and Horssina are racing each other once the moons are up."

"Really?" Prak trotted to the cave entrance. "I would bet a side of lydik that Horssina will easily take that race."

"No chance!" Tog snapped back, "Likkop has four wings!" The pair lifted into the dark sky debating the practicality of four wings versus a bifurcated tail until they couldn't be heard any longer.

"Am I not to see Anna before I leave?" Hiro asked through narrowed eyes.

Priya tilted her triangular head. "Do you question my care of the human?"

"Of course not," Hiro thumped his tail. "I'd just like to explain to her where I'm going and how long I'll be gone."

"She knows."

Hiro took a step toward her. "Where've you been, Priya?" Priya stared at him without blinking. "Come on, I know you won't tell the likes of Prak, but you can tell me. Can't you?"

Priya turned toward the entrance as well. "I hear you've been back to the surface while I was away." The starry sky made her scales and eyes sparkle.

"I'm not as afraid of it as I used to be," Hiro said, joining her in the entrance.

She tilted her head up to him. "And why is that?"

He dipped his head toward the surface drifting in the distance. "Because I learned that it's not as terrifying as I thought."

Priya grunted then ran down the mountain. Hiro followed, chasing her lashing tail. Just as he thought he might catch her, she jumped from the bottom edge of the mountain, catching the wind with her unfurled wings. Hiro, of course, tumbled down the slope after her to plummet into the air at the bottom before opening his wings.

The pair pressed the air back, soaring into the night. Once Hiro caught himself, a warm spring breeze allowed them to settle into a glide down the Inner Mountain and above the trees beyond. The scent of fresh new leaves on the trees felt tangy in Hiro's nose. Not the same tang of Kingstor Noble; it was a much sweeter scent there. Anna had much the same scent.

"I had unfinished business in the Desert Ruck," Priya said, jarring Hiro out of his thoughts.

He glanced sideways at her. "You couldn't tell Tog that before you disappeared on him?"

"I didn't think I needed to answer to anyone."

Hiro pressed his wings harder. "You do realize how worried everyone has been about you?" It wasn't really a question.

Priya shifted her eyes away from him. "I didn't know Tog cared so much."

Hiro dipped underneath her on a current to meet her eyes on the other side. "I wasn't talking about Tog."

She looked away again.

They flew in silence until Hiro enflamed his courage. "What news of Anna?"

"The human?" Priya glared at him.

Hiro's eyes drifted to the trees. "I gave her my wyrd she wouldn't be harmed."

"Why would you do such a foolish thing?"

Hiro rolled his shoulder. "I believe it benefits the entire ruck to return her safely." His eyes snapped to Priya. "She's okay, isn't she?" When she only continued to glare at him through narrowed eyes, Hiro ground his teeth together. "If she gets even a small scratch on her, Philip will tear through the Rock Clouds with faerie majik. Have you seen what he's done? Have you heard any of the reports? Your father's anger will seem a pleasant dream compared to Philip's wrath!"

Priya's face didn't twitch. "The woman is perfectly well." After pausing she added, "I'm well too, thanks for asking."

"How could a human harm you?" Hiro asked without thinking.

"Since the moment I returned, all you seem to care about me is where I've been," she growled.

"I could see with my own eyes that you're well."

"You didn't ask if I'd been hurt. Maybe that's why it took me so long to return!" she snapped at him.

"Is it?"

"No."

"Then why would you—?"

"You didn't ask, though, did you?" she barked. "No, all you seem to be concerned about is your little pet human."

"Priya, you know I..." He couldn't finish the thought. All his life he, Tog, and the other dans had been taught to guard their hearts. "Don't let it break until you have no other choice," their dans would tell them. "Don't let a dame steal your heart too young;" "don't let a dame control you unless she's good;" "don't allow a dame your heart unless you know she's worthy." On they would go, counsel and advice all leading to the same thing— "Guard your heart."

Lore among the dans indicated that a dan's heart would only break if two things came into sync with a third. First, a dan must think about the dame. He must consider her good qualities and bad. Second, he must love her for those qualities. A dan can feel his heart harden for a dame. Most of the time, he can choose to soften his heart against her, but sometimes it's not possible. And third, the most unproven step, the dame must be present.

As Hiro flew alongside Priya, he thought about all those things. He knew she was a worthy dame. He knew he would be proud of his heart breaking for her. She was strong, smart, just, loyal, and a dozen other wonderful qualities. Thinking of these, he felt into his heart. It hardened ever so slightly, then softened once again.

"Down there," Priya dipped her wing and headed south, descending at a slow angle.

"That's not the site I came upon," Hiro said. They were easily a half-day's flight from the Black Forest attack site.

"No," Priya whispered, "after you returned, Sarachi reported this one."

Hiro followed Priya into the trees. They brushed past the tender leaf shoots into a small clearing. Once his own claws were a claw length above the ground, Hiro closed his eyes. Both dragons landed with no more sound than the growing leaves.

He heard night bugs creeping over an old log, a small furry creature darting away from the newly arrived dragon threat, and several rapid beating hearts of small birds in the trees. No danger. When he opened his eyes, he saw Priya watching him.

"What are you doing?" she whispered into the stillness of the forest.

"Checking if I can hear anything nearby," he whispered back.

"Rakgar didn't give you this assignment because of your hearing," she rolled her eyes at him. "He gave it to you because of your vision."

Hiro's feeling of guilt for not telling her his most embarrassing secret gnawed at him. All the other dragons in the ruck, with the exception of Tog, thought Hiro had the best night vision of them all due to his night-black scales. Unfortunately, his scales belied the truth. His night vision was worse than that of almost every other dragon. But he made up for it with a keen sense of smell and even keener hearing.

He noticed Priya studying the ground around them. Once he inspected it closer, he saw the same kind of gray patches he and Anna had stumbled upon in the Black Forest.

"They're laid out in the same pattern," he said, treading carefully between the patches.

"What pattern?"

"They're in a circle." He indicated the pattern with his front claw.

Priya sunk low to the ground. "They were sleeping."

"Same as the ones I found."

She narrowed her eyes at him. "You and the woman."

"Her name is Anna."

"What do I care?"

Hiro reached into one of the piles of ash. "These remains aren't so low," he said. "They must have been in a hurry to leave, not to take as much as they could."

"Probably because they're already so close to the Rock Clouds," Priya shrugged.

Hiro pretended to scan the ground closely, but breathed in steady, deep draughts. "No," he pointed to the ground when he caught the scent, "centaurs."

"They interrupted," she said, nodding. "Good. If only they had come sooner."

Priya crawled around the piles snaking between them, looking for any more clues. But Hiro reached into one of the piles, scratching at the remains with his claws. "Are you looking for something?" she asked when she noticed what he was doing.

He didn't answer until he found what he was looking for. From the cooled embers he removed a nondescript arrow. Hiro laid it across his claws and bathed it with fire. The ash fell away as if it had been doused in water, but there remained on the point of the arrow the same black substance Anna had discovered.

Priya snatched the arrow out of his claw. "A single arrow? To kill four dames while they slept? How is this possible?"

"A single arrow for each," Hiro clarified. "But only one was necessary, I'm assuming. Anna and I found the same thing." He left out the part that Anna had also discovered the additional coating on the arrowhead. "Whatever is on these arrows must be deadly poisonous to dragons."

Priya's eyes bulged and her claw dropped the arrow. "Dragon poison?"

"It's the only explanation."

"But how? The only thing that..." she didn't finish the thought. The only thing that could harm a dragon was the flarote bulb. The small, round, reddish mushroom, named "the burning mushroom" for the fact that it was shaped like fire frozen in time, was the only thought in the dragons' minds.

Priya shook her head. "How could it be possible? They would have to—"

"—eat it," Hiro finished for her. "I know. Perhaps King Philip and the faeries are planning more than we realized."

"Maybe we should interrogate that human while we have her."

Hiro's face whipped around to meet Priya's. "You will not harm her."

Priya's eyes narrowed dangerously. "Why do you protect her so?"

"For the good of the ruck."

"Liar." Priya straightened from her attack stance. "I can always tell when you are lying, Hiro."

Hiro straightened from the attack stance he hadn't known he'd assumed. "There's nothing new to learn here."

He turned to leave, but Priya sat back on her haunches, peering into the night sky. "Are you a blood and ash traitor, Hiro?"

This time Hiro growled at her before assuming the attack posture.

She twisted her head over her shoulder to look at him. "I only ask because several others have asked me why your heart hasn't broken for me yet." Hiro had to fight to keep his maw from dropping open, but he couldn't stop his eyes from popping. Priya resumed her gaze at the stars. "A majishun once told me that it would."

She looked beautiful in the moonlight. As straight and still as one of the trees around her. Smooth and green as the newly growing leaves. Her tail drifted across the forest floor, away from the remains of her sister-dames. Hiro reached into his heart again. Again, it tightened and compacted at the alluring sight of her. And again, the more he willed it to happen, the faster it softened and the feeling melted away. It reminded him of trying to stab a snork without its spiky shell. The slippery slime surrounding one always let a snork squirm away.

He loped toward her, his mind warring between words of comfort and words of justification, but something else jumped to his mind. "Majishuns!" he stopped mid-stride and met her questioning eye. "The arrow!"

He bounced back to the piles of ash and dug through one of them again with both claws. Priya slithered next to him. "We need to take it to a majishun to find out what it is!" Once he found another arrow, he held it out to Priya.

She jerked the arrow from his claw and shook it at him. "Wait, we can't let any more faeries know about this poison."

He shook his head and pushed past her. Once again pretending to look at the ground, but sniffing it as he brushed past, he found the centaur scent again. "I have no intention of visiting faeries."

10

EMPIRICAL CONCLUSIONS

Crawling through the forest took much longer than flying over it, especially while carrying the arrow. They avoided large and dangerous creatures. They did take turns flying overhead to rest their legs. But Hiro had to remain on the ground to lead the way during any dark hours.

Once Priya signaled from the ground for Hiro to land and he found she'd killed a meikrat—part-lizard, part-mammal, and as long as Hiro's tail. They shared the meal before Priya launched into the sky and Hiro took lead again.

They came upon one herd of centaurs, but found no majishuns with them. The dragons were sent quickly on their way after suggesting such a thing. Centaurs didn't like faeries and faeries tended to use majik more than any other species. Therefore, majik wasn't looked kindly upon by the centaurs. But use it they did.

"Rylan?" one tall, shaggy centaur with enormous front teeth answered when Hiro inquired after the only centaur majishun he knew. "I believe he's traveling with his sister, Ashel. They stay much closer to the Noble Kingdom these days. You can find them on this side of the Torthoth Mountains. Probably just north of the Black Forest."

After another day of flying, the pair of dragons landed at the edge of the Black Forest. Hiro scoured the ground with his eyes and nose, since it was just past the peak of day. But it was Priya who found the hoofprints in the dirt leading into the foreboding trees.

Hours later the two dragons crossed a small stream. The trees on the other side twisted at the base before snaking into the dimming sky. Black leaves hung from dark red branches sagging overhead. Hiro could smell the centaur trail and even heard a few faint heartbeats, but he couldn't imagine why they would come to this murky place. Something whistled through the leaves.

"This place feels wrong," Priya whispered. "We should go around it."

The strange colors of the trees seemed to pull at Hiro's eyes. The sun dimmed as it set and the contorted trees and branches reaching toward the dragons made Hiro want to run. But he forced himself to continue. "They're nearby," he said in a low voice. "I don't want to miss them just because we get a strange feeling from trees."

"How do you know they're nearby?" she asked, but Hiro didn't listen to the rest of her question or her argument for going around.

He heard hooves beating the ground, two pairs flanking them and one coming straight at them.

"Quiet!" he whispered as loud as he dared to halt Priya's tirade. "They're coming."

She narrowed her eyes into the trees around them, but said nothing. Hiro stared straight ahead until a black shadow melted through the black tree trunks. When the tall black centaur came into view Hiro released his breath.

"Vikal!" he said with relief.

"Well met, Hiro!" Vikal, although an imposing centaur with a scar running across his face and onto his shoulder and arm, hailed Hiro by touching his nose-bridge and clapping his hands together. "Ashel claimed we would be seeing you soon. I think she was hoping your friend Prak would be with you."

Hiro grinned remembering how Prak had made a fool out of himself when he first met the beautiful leader of the warrior centaurs, Ashel. "Not this time," he said, saluting with the three-tiered centaur greeting of touching forehead, nose-bridge, and chest. "Instead I bring the daughter of Rakgar, Priya."

"Ah," Vikal exclaimed at the sight of her, "a dame! A true warrior comrade! And beautiful as well!" He saluted her with a light touch to his nose-bridge and bent his neck to her.

"Well met, Vikal," Priya said, delivering the three-tiered salute flawlessly. "May I meet this Ashel I've heard so much about?"

When Vikal turned back to go into the trees, Hiro saw two of the other four centaurs that had accompanied him to meet the visitors. One was gray with white dapples on her hind end, the other an orange-brown much redder than Ashel and her brothers. Neither centaur greeted the dragons. They watched from a distance before they turned to melt back into the trees. Hiro never saw to whom the other two sets of hooves belonged, nor did he learn how they had known he and Priya were approaching.

"What are you doing in such a place, Vikal?" Priya asked as they followed the intimidating centaur deeper into the forest under the black and red trees. "Why would anyone stay here?"

"It keeps out unwanted visitors," Vikal glared at the disquieting trees. "I'm sure you felt the effects of this place. We use it because the humans avoid it. We can camp here and track any humans without worry that they might stumble upon our camp. We've destroyed many of their feeble traps and in some cases the humans too."

"Why would you go to so much trouble to help dragons?" Priya asked.

Vikal glanced at her from the corners of his eyes. "If we don't defend our allies, then we will be forced to defend ourselves from more enemies."

Priya nodded with a thoughtful look.

The three entered the camp to shouts of welcome from the surrounding centaurs. Hiro was afraid that Ashel and the others might not be as friendly after his last meeting with the centaurs, at which they had had to prove their loyalty. But Ashel stepped out of a branch-laden shelter and greeted both dragons with a warm smile.

Her smile only added to the beauty of her face, with enormous eyes three times the size of a human's. She had woven more feathers and beads into the black, mane-like hair running down her back, and she had gone so far in ornamenting her appearance as to wrap three braids around her head, securing them with a strip of fur that hung over her ear.

Her brother, Rylan, stepped out of another shelter. Smoke drifted heavily from his thatched roof and it was much larger than Ashel's. Although he still didn't smile at them—Hiro had yet to see the centaur smile—he seemed much more at ease than the last time they met. Rylan's hair hung around his face, loose and untamed. Hiro immediately noticed the absence of the shining silver sword from his back.

Once introductions were made, Ashel gazed up at Hiro. "What brings you to us this time, my friend? I hope you're not in trouble again."

Hiro lifted the arrow in his claw. Holding it out, he proffered it to Rylan. "I was hoping your brother could help us identify the substance on this arrow."

She shook her head in amusement as Rylan picked up the arrow. "Why can't you just visit like a normal creature?" She said.

"It wouldn't be interesting if he didn't bring an element of danger with him," Vikal said with a sly grin.

With a mischievous grin of her own toward Vikal, Ashel responded, "Perhaps you should bring Prak to visit sometime. He would liven up the place." The glower she received from Vikal only made her grin spread. Hiro couldn't make sense of it.

"This might take some time, Hiro." Rylan seemed unaware of any conversation around him. He concentrated on the arrow in his hand. Scratching the forged metal head, he yelped when his finger slipped. Pulling the sliced finger away from the arrowhead, he watched it for a moment.

"Are you alright, Rylan?" Ashel asked, stepping closer to him.

"I'm fine," he answered. His brow creased, but he turned his finger to face her. "It healed almost instantly."

Upon closer inspection, everyone could see the droplet of blood left behind from the cut, with the healed skin underneath.

Ashel spun to face Hiro. "Where did you get this arrow?"

"Arrows like these are being used to kill dragons," he told her. "This was found in the remains of a dragon that was killed while she slept."

Ashel jerked back and shook her head, "That's impossible. You can't kill a dragon with a single arrow, or even a dozen arrows at once."

Priya put her head closer to Ashel's. In a low voice, she said, "We're no longer certain of that."

Rylan practically tumbled into his shelter. "I'll get to work on this," he shouted over his shoulder at them.

Ashel's eyes blazed at Priya. "What's going on? Humans are hunting and setting traps for dragons, then hauling away the embers. We've caught them at it. They get bolder and closer to the Rock Clouds every day. Why? What are they doing?"

"That's what we've come to find out," she answered.

Ashel's shoulders shook, but centaurs didn't get cold easily. She waved her hand toward her little shelter. "Please," she said, "we should share details."

The far side of the shelter had an opening large enough for Priya and Hiro to insert their heads. The rest of their bodies lay next to each other on the ground outside. Inside, the conversation was low and grim.

Hiro and Priya relayed to Ashel and Vikal the reports of dead hunting parties. Some had been attacked while awake; some had been killed while asleep, like the two Hiro saw. About half of the dragons killed had been killed instantly with a single arrow.

"Rupika said she saw one of the huntresses in her group die when a single arrow pierced her hide," Priya told the centaurs. "That's never been possible. Everyone assumed she missed something or her judgment was clouded in some way. I'm beginning to believe her."

"We haven't seen any strange black arrows," Ashel told her. "In fact," her eyes narrowed at Vikal, "I haven't seen any arrows. Have you?"

Vikal's already grim face blackened as he shook his head. "What does it mean?"

"I'm not sure," Ashel turned her attention back to Priya, "but the movement of the humans has grown bolder. In the beginning, just a handful of farmers or soldiers would appear to scrape up the remains of a random dragon killed in a forest." She glanced at Vikal. "We could usually just scare them away. But now they come in stronger numbers. If we scare them away, they come back a day or two later.

"Soldiers are coming deeper into the Black Forest in larger groups. Some of them are avoiding the Black Forest and setting up camps in the forest next to the Rock Clouds. We decided to set up camp here and run patrols along the Torthoth Range to try to safeguard the dragons in the Rock Clouds. But we can't keep up with all of them."

"You've done more than your share," Priya answered. "We'll have to warn all hunting parties to not go out alone and be extra vigilant to avoid any and all humans. I would suggest your group fall back under the Rock Clouds. We'll limit our hunting areas and perhaps include centaur escorts as well."

"We would be honored," Vikal nodded, "but there's a problem with those arrows." Ashel and Priya turned toward him and he continued. "Although that substance may heal us quickly, it could be a detriment if the arrow is already embedded."

"Of course," Ashel's head hung as she considered the consequences.

"I don't understand," Priya darted between the two of them. "What's wrong with something that heals you?"

Ashel scuffled her hooves. "If a body heals with an arrow in it, either the organs it passes through will stop working properly, or—"

"—or if they are somehow avoided and they continue to work, then taking the arrow out could cause more damage and the body may not heal as quickly," Vikal finished.

Hiro nodded, "So a little cut from the arrow is harmless. An arrow through the chest—"

Ashel sighed, "Possibly more fatal than a regular arrow."

"Ashel!" Rylan's voice outside cut through the dense silence inside. He pushed his head through the opening. Looking around at all of them, he said, "You need to see this."

Once the two centaurs and two dragons had extricated themselves from the cramped hut, Rylan led them to his own shelter. The camp had gone very quiet. The outside fires had been doused or burnt down to smoldering.

The dragons pushed around to the back of Rylan's shelter where another opening was sized properly for them. But Rylan stopped Vikal before he entered through the front. "I'm sorry, Vikal," he said, "but this information must be kept within as small a group as possible."

Vikal nodded and trotted back to the dark and quiet camp.

Ashel's eyes blazed at her brother. "I can make my own decisions about whom to trust, Rylan."

Her brother pointed a finger at her. "Not about this."

The four of them ducked inside the larger shelter to find it was almost as large inside as Hiro's lair. One wall was covered with hanging bags, each bag a different shape or size or color. A stone table was built next to the fire pit in the center of the large room, with a wooden table on the other side. A few pointed instruments and some dishes surrounded the dissected arrow in the middle of the wooden table.

Ashel looked around with tightened lips. "You know the others get nervous when you use majik."

Rylan waved the comment away. "The others get nervous around me because I can do majik, whether I use it or not."

Indicating the abnormally large space for the size of enclosure, Ashel said, "This doesn't help matters."

"I need the space. Besides," he pointed to the table in the middle, "you need to see this." Once everyone was comfortably inside, Rylan loped around the edges of the enclosure and unrolled silk hangings from the top to drape the walls. When the last one dropped he faced his sister. "Now no one will be able to hear us." Ashel just rolled her eyes and turned to the table.

"I knew the humans were gathering dragon ash," he said, picking up one of the three pieces of the arrowhead. The piece he held had been stripped of the black residue. "So I assumed they were using it in some way to their advantage. I was able to isolate the ash, but it evaporated, leaving behind a sticky red paste."

He put down the piece of arrow and picked up a length of metal rod with a red substance on its tip. "I couldn't figure out what it was until I thought about the potential healing properties."

He pointed to Hiro. "Does flarote heal dragons the way it heals other animals?"

Hiro glanced at Priya. He wasn't sure how much to reveal. The one and only secret the dragons still held from faeries, centaurs, and everyone else was the fact that while eating flarote would indeed heal them, eating too much flarote would kill them. Rylan now danced dangerously close to this discovery.

Priya stepped forward. "Of course it heals us like other animals. But doesn't it harm humans and centaurs? How could the substance have been flarote when your finger was healed from it?"

"True," Rylan nodded, "flarote is a deadly poison to centaurs. But I think mixing it with the dragon ash must change the composition enough to give it the opposite effect. This…" he picked up a small dish made of dragon scale. There was only a drop of red liquid in it. "This is the condensed oils of the flarote bulb, I'm sure of it. It holds the equivalent power of forty flarote bulbs."

Priya and Hiro jerked their heads away from it. Forty bulbs! Only half of that drop would kill both dragons and more! The centaurs noted their sudden movement.

Ashel eyed the dragons. "What aren't you telling us? Why would something that heals you make you react like that?"

Both dragons inspected the floor. Finally, Priya broke the silence. "It is a secret we have never divulged."

"Priya!" Hiro snapped at her. How could she imagine telling anyone?

"They must know, Hiro," she snapped back. Turning back to the centaurs, she said, "You must swear never to tell another soul."

The centaurs only glanced at each other before Ashel stood up straight. "We will never tell a soul. You may take our lives and those we tell if we break it. We both swear." Rylan jerked his head in agreement without a hint of hesitation.

Priya bit her lip then whispered, "If a dragon eats too much flarote, it will kill them. Yes, it heals, but too much kills. It's a delicate balance."

Rylan nodded. "It makes sense; other herbs and elements do the same thing to centaurs, humans, and even faeries."

Hiro thought of an earlier riddle game he had played with Anna. "You can swallow it and it can swallow you," he muttered to himself.

"What swallows you?" Priya asked.

"Water…" Hiro met the eyes of the others, "even water can be good and bad."

She lilted her head. "Is that a riddle?"

"Yes," he answered. "I remember it from playing with—" he snapped his jaw shut, blinked, then smiled to cover the hesitation, "—someone a few sun cycles ago."

Priya narrowed her eyes at him, but said nothing.

"Riddles aside," Rylan interjected, "there are so many herbs in all of Avonoa, and numerous combinations of those herbs, that no one can know if others might exist that can harm you as well. What we do know is that someone, and I think we all know who the culprit in this situation might be, has discovered a dragon poison."

Ashel crossed her arms against her chest. "We must inform Joss." Her eyes shot to Priya's. "Do we have your permission?"

Priya nodded.

"He's gathering centaurs now to help combat the human threat to the dragons…" Ashel's lips pursed in a tight line and her large eyes focused on something far away.

"He is?" Hiro asked, but his question was passed over.

"He must be informed," Ashel continued, stamping one of her front hooves. "We'll have to organize. Try to find where and how they're producing it. We'll have to send search parties into the Noble Kingdom. Strategic strikes to distract as well as dissuade…" her voice faded into mutters to herself.

"But—" Hiro started, but Rylan shook his head.

"It's no use," the centaur told Hiro, "she's gone into combat mode. She'll be distracted until something more important comes up."

"We're fortunate to have such allies," Priya told him, but then turned to Hiro. "We must get this information back to my father." She nodded to Rylan, "I don't mean to be rude, but we should take our leave. Immediately."

"I understand." He trotted back to the large opening meant for the dragons, lifted the curtain for them, and followed them out. "We'll try to send you any additional information we can discover. Until then—"

"Hiro!" Ashel shouted behind them. She trotted up to the dragons, but cast a sidelong glance at Priya. "A moment, please?"

Hiro nodded. "You can say anything in front of Priya."

Ashel nodded as well, but when she met his eyes they burned into him. "Do you remember the conversation we had when we first met? About the stars?"

Hiro's brow compressed. "You warned me about the faeries and humans threatening me. You also warned me of a dangerous creature. I think I've already met that one."

Ashel shook her head. "This is something else." She stepped closer and her eyes burned brighter. "Five stars are converging. Many centaurs have conjectured on the meaning. I believe it means war. I have been watching your star, Hiro, and I've seen many things. But the most meaningful is the convergence of these five stars. They're all converging on your star, Hiro."

Hiro pulled his head away slightly. "What does it mean?"

"You—" Ashel's voice shook with what Hiro assumed to be fury, as this centaur couldn't possibly feel fear. "You will be at the center of a war between the five kingdoms of Avonoa. You might be what they fight over or for or about, but I know you'll be at the heart of it. Hiro," she straightened to stare him in the eye, "when the time comes, the centaurs will follow you." She glanced at Priya and back at Hiro. "Only you."

"Ashel," Hiro leaned down to her, "I have no intention of being in any war."

"No one ever does."

11

NOTIONS OF ASSURANCE

"Murzod's late again," Torgon grumbled, slouching through the door into the king's office. "He's trying to set a precedent. He wants to show me that he doesn't have to answer to me." Instead of sitting, like usual, the Royal General paced the length of the office.

"Shouldn't we have had two reports by now?" Philip asked. He didn't really keep up with how often the reports were supposed to arrive, but felt the lack.

"We should have had a third arriving tomorrow, but the messenger just arrived and—" Torgon threw his hands in the air. He stopped pacing. "I don't trust him."

"Neither do I," Philip leaned back in his chair, "but what can we do?"

"I'm going up there."

Philip bolted from his chair. "No, you're not!"

"Someone has to go and no staff guard or messenger can demand straight answers."

"Your position is here. In Kingstor." Philip leaned over his desk.

"It's my duty to protect the men in my charge and this kingdom—"

"—and me!" Philip shouted.

Torgon shook his head. "You don't need me here to protect you. Good men that can be trusted will remain here. Besides, you're perfectly capable of protecting yourself."

"You can send someone else! Tommak, or one of your captains!" Philip's voice rose uncomfortably, but he pressed further. "A dragon has taken my sister! We're under threat again! You can't just leave!"

"You know I wouldn't argue with you but Murzod is going to need stern convincing of my authority."

"There are more pressing matters here!"

Torgon continued talking to himself, resuming his pacing, as if Philip weren't there. "He won't take that from just anyone."

"Tommak is more than capable!"

"No, I'll need to go up there and make an example of him."

"The journey alone is treacherous!" Philip tried to control his voice. He couldn't lose another friend.

Torgon waved the comment away. "I'll be well provisioned."

"But the dragon!" Philip insisted.

"Take an armed guard wherever you go. You can do more with that bow of yours than I would be able with my sword. If I take a smaller, faster party, we can be to the halfway point in less than a fortnight and they have much faster means of communication with the northern party."

"What if I need your help here?" Philip couldn't sit there and allow his closest friend to run into the arms of danger.

"What would you need my help with that Tommak can't do?"

Philip paused. An idea struck him, but he hesitated.

Noticing the silence, Torgon turned back to the king. "Everything will be fine. I'll be back in a month or so and—"

"Help me find a queen."

Torgon's mouth hung open midsentence.

Philip stood up straighter. "Anna was right. I need to focus on producing an heir. If the worst has happened to Anna, it's become even more important."

The corner of Torgon's mouth curled up. "I can arrange a formal court introduction."

Philip flopped into his chair.

———

"Rakgar!" Hiro clattered into Rakgar's lair. He and Priya had flown all night to reach the Rock Clouds. Now they had pushed past Prak and Tog and The Watch without a word. Prak and Tog and a few other dragons followed them into the spacious cave. "We must speak to you. It's urgent!"

"What is it?" Rakgar pushed past Milah to meet Hiro and Priya. "What's happened?"

"We found the ashes, the same way—"

The faerie Skorkot stepped out from behind Milah.

Hiro snapped his jaw shut. Lowering himself to the floor, he bared his fangs. "What is she doing here?"

"Hiro," Rakgar rumbled at him, "how dare you treat my guest this way?"

Priya crouched beside him. "Faeries are liars and murderers."

Skorkot's blood visibly pulsed through her veins, making them bulge. If her skin were opaque her face would've flushed with anger. "How dare you?" She rose into the air with the humming of her wings.

"Skorkot, please," Rakgar tried to appeal to her.

"I will not listen to this abuse." Her silver hair fluttered about her face in the breeze from her wings. Her hands contorted into claws with her palms turned to Hiro.

"Then leave, beast," Hiro growled.

"Hiro!" Rakgar leapt at the smaller dragon. With his nose inches from Hiro's, his hot breath swept over Hiro's face. "Apologize. Now."

Hiro pried his eyes from the faerie to bore them into Rakgar. "I'll do no such thing. And I'll not say another word in front of that monster."

"Nor will I," Priya echoed at his side.

Rakgar pulled his head away from Hiro. He studied Priya through narrowed slits in his eyes. Finally, he shifted his head to Skorkot. "Skorkot, will you please give me a moment to chastise these younglings."

Hiro growled in the back of his throat.

The faerie's claws relaxed. Without a word, she flew into the passageway far in back on the opposite side of the entrance to Priya's lair. At least Hiro could be sure she wasn't down there abusing Anna.

Once she disappeared, Hiro sat up out of his attack posture. "Prak, would you please make sure the faerie doesn't listen to our conversation?"

While Prak ran over to the entrance to Rakgar's private lair, he scooped up a large rock and breathed flame on it to make it glow. Setting it and himself at the entrance, Hiro knew he would be the one listening and watching.

"Have you returned your mind?" Rakgar bellowed rounding on the pair. "The faeries are our allies! They always have been!"

"No longer," Hiro whispered.

Between the two of them, Hiro and Priya related, through both words and memories, all that had happened on the surface. They told Rakgar about finding the circle of dragon ashes, the single arrow embedded in the leftover ash, the small piles from someone collecting the ash, the visit to the centaurs, and the discovery of the dragon poison.

"It's not possible," Rakgar rumbled low. "The centaurs would blame the faeries and the faeries would blame the centaurs. You can't trust them."

"We can't trust the centaurs, but we can trust the faeries?"

"Skorkot is an old friend, Hiro," Rakgar shook his head. "Even if a few faeries did create some evil plot—which I don't believe—we can still trust the faeries we know."

"Has she investigated any of the incidents I've reported to you?" Hiro asked. "Kradik's treatment of me? The wraith? Anything?"

Rakgar shrugged. "She reported everything to the Faerie Council and I'm sure they're looking into it. She hasn't investigated anything herself because she is here to advise me."

Hiro twitched his tail. "Advise you on what?"

"Everything. Anything. Especially what to do about that little human you're so fond of."

Priya snorted.

Hiro inspected the eyes of the dragons around him. Rakgar, tall and proud. Someone he had always looked up to. Milah, he didn't care what Milah thought. Tog and Prak, good friends. One of them knew his every secret anyway. Priya, who could read him like script on a wall at most times. Other dragons were behind him, but he didn't know them, nor did he care. He froze. "I would trust that woman before I would ever trust a faerie again."

If Skorkot had invisibly snuck in at that moment, the silence in the cave would have echoed her footsteps.

"You can't mean that." Rakgar's whisper seemed a roar. "They tortured you."

"Not Anna." Hiro looked meaningfully into Rakgar's eyes.

Rakgar also pondered the faces around them. "I see," he said, turning back to Hiro. He nodded to himself, crawling next to the wall. The mighty, gray dragon curled himself on the floor but then sat straight up to his fullest height. When he faced Hiro again, pure hatred burned behind his eyes. "I will discuss circumstances with my advisors and send you word of my decision." Milah sat next to Rakgar and glared at Hiro with a smug expression. "You're dismissed, Hiro Tekla."

Hiro couldn't believe it. Rakgar dismissing him like he owned the mountain! Hiro sat up as straight as he could. "I want to see the human. I can return her now."

"You'll leave before I name you blood and ash traitor!" Rakgar bellowed.

Hiro ran from the cave.

———

Curled on the floor of his own cave, Hiro listened to his friends arguing over him.

"What were you thinking?!" Tog yelled.

"He was only saying what he believed!" Prak asserted for Hiro.

"To admit that you would trust a human?!"

"I admit, it's a little unorthodox."

"Unorthodox? Prak, its blasphemy!"

"Why?"

"Why? WHY?!"

Silence.

Hiro looked up when the two fell quiet. Tog's face was perplexed and Prak looked smug.

"Think about it," Prak pranced around almost on tip-talons. "We can't speak to humans, but that doesn't mean we can't trust them. If one of them had a knife to us, we could resist or allow ourselves to fall into their hands. If we were hurt or injured," Tog and Hiro shared a glance, "we might have to subject ourselves to them for healing.

We might have no other choice. Like a pet. Or a common wild animal. Either way, is it really that bad to trust a human?"

"The other choice is to die," Tog muttered. "Any decent dragon would rather."

"Oh? Is it wrong to choose to live? Hiro doesn't trust faeries because he has evidence that he believes proves them to be murderers and liars. If he chooses not to trust them and chooses to avoid the danger, is that ignorance? Or blasphemy?"

"Prak, you don't understand—"

"No," Hiro looked at Tog, "I think he understands better than most."

Tog grumbled and turned away. As they sat in silence—which was rare for Prak—Priya's voice echoed outside.

"Hiro!" she called, landing at a run inside his cave. "How could you be so stupid?"

"Is it stupid to speak the truth?" Prak piped from his side.

"Here we go again," Tog grumbled, rolling his eyes and flopping his head on his claws.

"Is it stupid to stand up for what you believe? Is it stupid to—"

"Snap it, worm!" Priya barked at the small brown dragon. "I'm speaking to you, Hiro. Not your little shadow."

"Why not?" he turned away, pulling his claws over his head. "He can say things much better than I can."

Prak sniffed. Hiro could sense the pride in it, but Priya pushed past him. "My father has given you permission to come get the woman." Hiro's head whipped around. "Ah, I see I finally have your attention."

Hiro jumped to his feet. "Did you bring her or can I go get her now?" He searched around Priya as if to find Anna materialized.

Hiro could see Priya's jaw working. Without parting her grinding teeth or taking her eyes from Hiro, she said, "Tog, Prak, would you please give us a moment?"

Tog loped out of the cave without a backward glance, but Prak hesitated. Hiro nodded to him before he finally slipped out.

"You may get her at dawn," Priya stated. He still wasn't sure her teeth had unclenched.

"Is that all?"

"No." But she only stared at him.

"If you have something else to say, then say it. I'd like to get some sleep before I have to travel again." He laid his head on his claws again.

"I'll be leaving again soon. I'll be gone before you get back."

His head pricked up. "Where are you going?"

Priya turned to leave. "Does it matter? I'll be gone a long time again."

"Priya!" When she stopped, he shook his head to clear it. "I'm sorry I've disappointed you. You of all others."

She sighed, "Don't believe everything that woman tells you, Hiro."

His brows creased. "Anna?"

"She's a liar." Priya's breathing quickened. "She's lied to you before and she'll do it again."

"How do you know?"

Priya snapped her tail. "She's human."

As Priya darted from the cave, Hiro inspected his heart. He should believe Priya. Her of anyone. But with its next beat, his heart softened again.

12

BAIT

"This is stupid," Philip grumbled, trying not to adjust the trappings around his throat. When Murthur heard of the endeavor, he brought in several maids to help choose the king's wardrobe for the formal court introductions. Murthur shooed them all out when one of them made a comment about a ball being the only proper way for the king to meet a woman.

The outfit they picked for him had so much gold stitching that Philip wasn't sure what color the material was supposed to be. "Show off the station!" they had insisted. Philip had immediately refused the shirt with the ruffled cuffs and neckline, but he couldn't talk Murthur out of the gilt belt and boot buckles.

He bowed and smiled as Lord Dieko (whom Torgon thought they should allow the honor) introduced another young woman. Lady Pramilla Ida Pracine gave a graceful curtsy in her blood-red gown; however, the neckline was so low that Philip had to glance away out of modesty. And when she looked up at him with a smile, he had to force one of his own. At more than twice his age and with only one eyebrow, he didn't have to wonder at her availability.

"We have more important things to worry about," he whispered to Torgon as she stepped down.

"I agree," he whispered back, "but until a dragon attacks the castle, we get news from Anna's search party, or you allow me to follow the men I sent, this is our first priority."

Dieko next introduced Lady Ellyn, who seemed pleasant as she curtsied. She was young and her hair wasn't puffed up as tall and ridiculously as that on most of the other women he'd met that day. Her face had the same amount of color applied, but it didn't seem as overpowering. Philip was surprised that a smile at her came more easily, although no other feelings presented themselves.

"Fine," he whispered again, "but when this is over I'm taking the rest of the day for target practice."

"Whatever you say, Sire," Torgon said through a smile at Lady Trikorna, "but it will take that much longer if you don't find someone you fancy, and we'll have to do this all over again tomorrow. Just
imagine," another smile and nod to Lady Loli—who couldn't have been more than twelve— "the moment women throughout the Noble Kingdom hear that you're meeting in court with all the eligible women, I'm sure your days will be filled with beauties like these."

Philip nearly groaned as Lady Ranika stepped forward and curtsied. "Are we going to do this every day until I find someone I like?"

Torgon smiled a genuine smile at Lady Haven. "A happy king makes for a happy kingdom."

Philip's forced cheeks began to ache. "Your father said that we make our own happiness."

"Yes, but he was married," Torgon sighed. "He got happiness all the time."

Philip's smile faltered.

———

An informal feast followed the formal court introductions. The feast hall tables were spread with crackers, cheeses, pastries, puffs, fruits, and row upon row upon row of wine goblets. Philip had to wonder whether Torgon or Murthur, or both, hoped to make him drunk so he would propose to a woman that day.

He picked up a wine goblet, but before it could touch his lips several gentlemen stepped toward him. Lord Juskin got to him first.

"Your Majesty," Juskin bowed his head, dipping the feather on top of his head into Philip's wine. "You've just met my daughter, Lady Ellyn." The indicated young woman appeared out of thin air beside Philip.

"Ah, yes," Philip answered. She did have pretty eyes. "Remind me what province you're from," he said as he took Ellyn's hand and bowed to her.

"Clearwater, Sire," Ellyn batted her eyes. "Just down Crying River from Kingstor. My father and I happened to be visiting when they announced the formal court introductions for today. So I insisted on staying for them."

She still hadn't let go of his hand.

"I'm so glad you were able to come," Philip said while trying in vain to subtly extricate his fingers.

"Would you like to take a walk in the garden, Sire?"

"Ellyn!" Juskin whispered sharply to quiet her before anyone could overhear her impropriety.

Her startled face made her eyes bulge and she finally released the king's hand at her father's admonition. "It's alright, Lord Juskin," Philip nodded. "Perhaps another time, Lady Ellyn." It would be just as improper for him to accept as it was for her to offer.

He turned from the pair to avoid the inevitable berating the daughter would receive for her actions. Three more lords stood behind him, waiting to push their daughters into his arms. Luckily for Philip, he was tall enough to see over all the heads of the men standing around him. Through the feathers and lace headdresses, he recognized the aged forehead on the man standing by the table.

Excusing himself before he could be cornered by any of the lords, Philip made his way over to the table. "Lord Sherped!" he exclaimed, greeting the elderly gentleman. Months ago, a horrible wrong had been committed. Sherped had been a villager brought before Philip, who was only a prince at the time. Philip recognized the wrong and made an example of Sherped's honesty by punishing two lords and giving their lands and titles to Sherped. Philip couldn't be happier to see the older man now in a finely made coat without gilt or embroidery, as handsome and simple as the man himself.

"I'm so glad you've come! I trust the situation in your village has improved under your leadership," Philip said, joining him next to the table.

The older man dropped a cracker with red sauce back onto the table plate and bowed to the king. "Yes, Sire." He haltingly met Philip's eye. "The people in Carpen Stream were very happy to hear of my appointment. I also had them put forward names of people to take the other title for the area, and a good man was chosen. Everyone is very pleased."

"Excellent!" Philip turned to the woman standing behind the elderly gentleman's shoulder. "Did you happen to bring someone to introduce at court today?"

When she stepped in front of him, Philip saw that the woman was wearing a dress made of sturdy green cloth with nothing but a bit of white lace for decoration atop her silver-gray hair.

"Name's Saryn, Your Majesty," the woman said with a lift of her chin. "And I held out of the introductions, seeing as you were looking for a younger woman, Sire."

She looked Philip straight in the eye and Philip smiled. Saryn's piercing gaze never wavered, but she also displayed smile lines around her mouth and eyes. Her hands were rough from hard labor and her eyes as discerning as a teacher's, but he could imagine her bouncing two grandchildren on each knee.

Dipping his chin to her, Philip whispered, "Only because a woman of your stature would never tolerate me."

At this Saryn's head tilted and her face softened. "Why are you looking for a wife now?"

"Saryn!" Sherped whispered, but she shushed him.

"Everyone wants to know," her penetrating gaze returned to Philip. "You're very young, you have time."

Philip pursed his lips. "If I may take you into my confidence," Saryn's eyes widened and she tilted her head closer, "my sister has disappeared again. If anything happened to her, I would be forced to rule the kingdom alone. If anything happened to me, Royal General Torgon would be forced to stand for me and he would dislike nothing more. Therefore, he's insisted I find a wife and produce an heir."

Saryn punched her hands onto her hips. "Politics." Sherped shook his head at the floor. "I should have known. Men think only of politics and logic."

Philip spread his hands in confusion. "Should I not look to the good of the kingdom?"

"No, you should not." Saryn's response was so prompt that Philip's eyebrows shot up to his hairline.

"But that's my duty as king."

"Yes," Saryn clarified, "your duty as king means you should do what's best for the kingdom. But your duty to yourself should come first. A happy king makes a happy kingdom." She echoed Torgon's words before wagging a finger at him. "I'm not saying you shouldn't find a wife. I'm saying you shouldn't have to force yourself to do it. Marry for love. Marry for happiness. All in due time."

That didn't help Philip prevent Torgon from charging head first into danger, but it made him grin nonetheless. "Yes, Lady Saryn, but you're not available."

"Then might I make a suggestion?" Saryn asked.

"Please, do." Philip noted Sherped shaking his head again.

Saryn's sweet smile hid behind sparkling eyes. "Don't look for physical beauty. Ugly personalities hide too easily behind beauty."

13

UNEXPECTED PUNISHMENT

Philip's head danced with Saryn's words as his feet worked their way around the room. He had to agree with her summation. The prettier the young lady, he sometimes found, the worse her personality. Although many didn't throw themselves at him as obviously as Lady Ellyn had, they often harbored superior attitudes and condescending opinions, and made overbearing remarks toward others.

After finishing one such conversation, where Lady Teel insisted that her servants kneel in her presence, Philip decided to put Saryn's guidance into action. Glancing around the room, he spied a young woman picking at the pastries on one end of the food table.

She was plain-looking. Utterly plain. Her blue dress displayed little gilt and embroidery, like many others he'd seen that day. Her brown hair twisted into ringlets at the top of her head and dripped down through intricate lace. Her face had more color added to it than others, perhaps to hide more flaws. Her eyes were a little too wide and she had a large gap between her two front teeth. Philip sidled toward her.

Leaning toward her as she lifted a small white pastry off the plate, he whispered, "Are they any good?"

Her response was astounding. The young woman yelped as if he'd stuck a pin in her back end then coughed on the bit of food already in her mouth. Other guests turned to inspect the commotion. Philip tried to ignore the stares at the scene he'd created. He pounded the choking lady on the back a couple of times before handing her a goblet of wine.

"I'm sorry," he said through her coughing fit, "I didn't mean to startle you."

"Startle me?" she coughed again, "you could have at least announced your—" her voice cut off when she finally looked up at him. "I mean, I didn't expect you to…no one ever…I'm so sorry." She coughed into a napkin again, took a sip of wine, and composed herself. "I'm sorry," she said again, "I didn't expect anyone to notice me. Least of all you."

"I don't recall you being introduced in court," he said with a formal bow.

She placed the goblet on the table and curtsied. "I'm Lady Coralee. I've been introduced at court before. I didn't think it was necessary to do it again."

"But I wanted to meet all the ladies of the kingdom. That includes you."

"Well," Coralee shrugged, "now you've met me. Again."

"Where are you from?" Philip searched his mind for questions to ask.

"I'm from Trillik province, in the east."

Philip nodded. "Have you been in Kingstor long?"

"No."

"What brought you to Kingstor?"

"My carriage." Coralee snorted and giggled, which brought on more coughing. She composed herself with another sip of wine.

Philip grinned, but when he glanced in a mirrored vase sitting on the table he saw three pairs of lords with their daughters waiting behind him.

Coralee peeked around his shoulder as well. "I'm sure you have many other people to talk to, My Lord."

Philip stood up straighter and replied, "Actually, I wonder if you'd mind accompanying me in the gardens?"

Coralee's jaw dropped in a very unladylike manner. Philip heard a small gasp behind him. But he turned elegantly on his heel and offered Coralee his arm. The noise in the hall dropped as, in haltingly slow motion, she wrapped one arm under his elbow.

She moved to set her goblet on the table, but Philip forestalled her. "You might need refreshment," he added, thinking of her coughing fits. Arm in arm, they stepped together out of the hushed hall.

Once away from the stuffy hall, Philip gave Coralee a genuine smile at remembering the look of pride on Saryn's face and shock on Torgon's as the young couple left.

Fortunately, the guards they passed were much more composed as they walked through the castle hallways. Unfortunately, Philip had to search for things to say.

"Are you visiting someone in Kingstor?" he asked, trying to renew the semblance of a conversation.

"My cousin," Coralee nodded.

After a pause, Philip asked, "Has your cousin been introduced in court?"

"Yes."

Another awkward pause.

"Might I inquire your cousin's name?" He fished for more conversation, but thought he might have an easier time of it with one of the guards.

"I'm sorry, it's Merik," she stuttered. "I should've said that. I'm visiting Lady Merik and her husband, Lord Calvin."

"I believe I've met Lord Calvin on a—"

"—guard promotion, yes!" Finally on a familiar subject, Coralee continued in detail about the guard promotion of someone in her family.

However, Philip didn't hear a word. At that moment, a young serving woman stepped from a side hall across the way. She met his eyes and didn't look away. Usually the servants in the castle and even commoners insisted their king not look them in the eye. Their eyes locked for a moment; his filled with wonder, but hers filled with…defiance…anger…impatience?

He had never seen her. Or maybe he had never allowed himself to swim in her sparkling, bright blue eyes before. Glossy, nearly black flyaway locks escaped the bun on her head to tickle her cheeks. Full lips pursed in a line as if the king and his guest were in her way.

Where could she be going? Philip thought. *What could be so important?*

But before a single thought could form into an idea in his head, the young woman spun on her heel and disappeared the way she'd come.

Wait! Philip cried in his head. *Who is she? Where did she come from? I can't exactly go asking after a servant girl!*

He shifted his attention back to young Coralee. She drifted silently next to him. Her finger tapped against his arm while she peered at the shields hanging along the wall.

He decided against feigning to have heard what she'd said. "Will you be warm enough if we go outside?" he asked.

She glanced down at her long sleeves. "I should be fine," she answered. "I was already getting too warm in the feast hall. I mean, not that it was too warm in there, it was perfect, but I seem to always be too warm, or warmer than most people. I don't usually need a cloak outside in the spring because I'm always so warm. My father insists that I wear a cloak outside, but I—" her mouth closed with a CLOP, then opened again. "I'm rambling. I apologize. I should be fine." She turned away and sipped her wine.

Philip grinned. "It's perfectly all right." Why couldn't he think of anything other than those blue eyes?

Think of something else to ask her! he berated himself about the woman next to him. *Where is she from? No, I know that about Coralee! She's from…from…those blue eyes!*

He couldn't think of anything else. Philip grinned down at Coralee as they turned a corner.

BLUE EYES!
BAM!
SPLASH!
CLATTER!

"I'm so sorry, my lady!" the young blue-eyed woman's cheeks burned red. Philip was so surprised to see her again that he didn't realize what had just happened. The servant's eyes were fixed on Coralee. When Philip heard her panting, he forced his attention back to the young woman he was escorting.

Coralee's face was red too, but not from embarrassment. Her empty wine goblet teetered on the floor, the contents running down Coralee's face, neck, and chest. Some had splashed on Philip's arm and clothes, but the rest ran onto her gown, turning it a deep purple.

The serving girl's shoulders dropped when she beheld the ruined sheets she held in her arms, but she dislodged one to attempt to wipe the lady's face. "I'm so sorry. I didn't hear you coming. I thought I would miss you if I went this way."

Coralee's face contorted. "Well, you didn't!" she shouted, snatching the sheet from the servant's hand. "Look what you've done!" she hollered at her own dress. "It's ruined! I had to wait a week for this material!"

Guards were starting to turn in their direction, but Philip waved them away. "Coralee, I'm sure the dress can be saved," he attempted to placate her.

"No, it can't!" she wailed louder, getting more looks from the guards. "I'll have to burn it and wait another week to get more material!"

"I work in the laundry," the servant said gently, "if you come with me, I'm sure Mistress Kay can take the wine straight out of it."

"I'm not going anywhere with you!" Coralee practically screamed, inviting heads to peek out at them from doorways, "I wouldn't trust the laundry mistress of a castle whose servants would do something like this!"

The blue-eyed servant's eyes flashed with anger, but Philip held his hand out to both women. "Now, Coralee—" Why did his voice have to catch now? "It was just an accident."

"Accident? ACCIDENT? This wretch attacked me on purpose! She saw us in the hallway and she was jealous! It was no accident!" Coralee's finger flew to within inches of the servant's face, but instead of flinching away from it, her long eyelashes lowered dangerously over her brilliant blue eyes.

Philip looked down at her, waiting for a reaction. However, the young servant flashed her eyes to Philip before casting them to the floor. "I did nothing of the sort, my lady, but I apologize for making a mess."

At this, Coralee folded her arms across her chest. "I don't believe it."

"Coralee," Philip tried to temper her.

"No," she shook her head, "I demand she be punished."

Philip tried not to gape. Coralee impatiently tapped her foot. The servant girl stood with her head bowed in silence. He shook his head at the whole situation.

Finally, Philip motioned for one of the guards to join them. "Please accompany Lady Coralee to the laundry and ask Mistress Kay to help her clean up," he told the staff guard. Then, turning to Coralee, he indicated the young servant and said, "I'll see to her punishment."

Coralee stuck her nose in the air and stormed off with the guard chasing her.

Once they had turned the corner, Philip sighed. Turning around, he found the servant on her hands and knees gathering the ruined sheets from the floor. "Come with me," he told her.

He spun to march down the hallway they had come from, but turned down a different hallway almost immediately. This smaller hall led past the feast hall and audience hall straight to his office. He forced himself not to check behind himself to see if she was following, or walk slower to wait for her. He used the servant hallways to avoid being seen by anyone except guards.

The last guards stood in front of his private office entrance. Not expecting him there that day, he had to wait for them to unlock and open the door. Whisking past them and inside, Philip threw himself into his chair behind his massive desk. Why hadn't he cleaned it up a little before he finished with Murthur yesterday?

Pursing his lips, he motioned for the young woman to sit in the chair opposite him.

What am I supposed to do with her?! He tried to keep a calm face. *I can't punish her, it was an accident!*

She squirmed in the chair, still holding the stained sheets, as he scrutinized her. It helped that she kept her focus on the ground, or the walls, or the sheets.

"What's your name?" Philip asked. Yes, that sounded innocuous.

"Tierni, Your Majesty," she said. She kept her voice low, but firm. He wondered if she had ever been afraid of anything in her life.

By Shurta, that's a beautiful name! Well, that was something, he thought, *now what do I do?* He stared at her some more. *It was intimidating, right?*

Once he felt the silence between them had gone on long enough, he asked, "Do you have anything to say for yourself?"

Her eyes pierced into his. *No,* he thought, *she has never been afraid of anything.*

"Nothing that hasn't already been said, Your Majesty."

He could feel the sun overhead in those eyes! He desired nothing more than to sit and stare into them.

Of course! Philip felt a surge of relief. *But how do I say it?*

The sound of shouting outside his door brought Philip out of his reverie.

"You let me in there or I'll make sure your breeches are never cleaned again!" the muffled sound came from the servant's entrance.

When he glanced at Tierni, she dropped her face into her hands and shook her head. He feared she might cry and he wouldn't know what to do then! So, he rose quickly to cross the room and open the door.

In the hallway stood the ever-feared Mistress Kay of the laundry, shaking her finger in the face of one of the guards. The guard had gone as far as pressing his back against the wall, but neither guard had made a move to open the door. Bravery in the face of danger.

Mistress Kay wore a sparkling white apron over her blue livery dress. Unlike the lesser servants that wandered the hallways in blue livery with a silver sword embroidered on the back, any master or mistress in charge of an area wore a silver sword on their left shoulder. The silver sword signified their belonging to the household of the Noble Kingdom. Her gray hair was pulled into a bun like Tierni's, but white wisps flew in several different directions instead of dangling delicately next to her face. Her cheeks were the color of the sunset, but Philip knew it had nothing whatsoever to do with embarrassment.

"Your Majesty," she dropped a deep curtsy, "I'm sorry to interrupt like this, but I must insist on speaking with you."

"Of course," he swept to the side to allow her to enter his office. "Come in, Mistress Kay."

Throwing one last nasty glare at the two guards in the hallway, she stepped into the room. She immediately positioned herself next to Tierni's chair with her nose in the air and her hands on her hips.

Once the door closed, Mistress Kay opened her mouth, but at the king's glance, she closed it.

"Has the Lady Coralee been seen to?" he asked the laundry mistress.

"Of course, Your Majesty," Mistress Kay lifted her nose higher in the air as if the question were an insult. "But I've come to talk to you about this one." She tossed her head at young Tierni sitting in the chair.

Philip swallowed, but hid his concern by seating himself behind his desk again. If Mistress Kay were this upset at the beautiful young servant, he might have to end up dismissing her. "Would you like to say something in her defense?" he prompted.

"Only this," Mistress Kay took a step toward him. "She's got a strong attitude, this one. She's bull-headed and often thinks herself above her station. She's got a sharp tongue and rarely tempers it."

Philip steepled his fingers in front of his chest. "This hardly sounds like a defense, Mistress."

"She's also the best laundry maid I've got." Mistress Kay bit her lip and glanced briefly over her shoulder to see Tierni lift her face to the older woman. "She's a hard worker and never shirks her duties. She never asks others to do her work and she willingly takes on that of others to help. She's learned quickly in the time she's been with me and I think she has the makings of a great mistress someday. She's never had an accident like this before and I refuse to think she did anything of the sort on purpose. I hate to admit it, but…I'd be lost without her." Mistress Kay wrung her hands. "I even went so far as to dissuade Princess Anna from taking her as a personal maid when she came looking for one."

Interesting, Philip thought, *she's a hard worker and willing to help others, but still considers herself equal to nobles.*

Philip nodded, "I promised Lady Coralee that I would see to her punishment personally."

"I'll take it." Philip blinked, not believing what he'd just heard. Tierni half-stood from her chair, but when she began to speak Mistress Kay pushed her back to sit and kept her hand on the girl's shoulder. "Quiet, girl," she told her, then turned back to the king. "I'll take her punishment myself," she repeated.

Philip inhaled deeply. "A mistress willing to take her inferior's punishment is indeed strong evidence against it. However," he held up a finger to forestall their questions, "I must insist on the worst possible punishment I can think of; and you will not be allowed to take her place, but you will be included in it." Mistress Kay tightened her lips and he saw her hand gently squeeze Tierni's shoulder. Tierni lowered her eyes beneath her long lashes. After an intentional, tension-filled pause, Philip sat up straight. "Mistress Kay, you will dress Tierni in the best gown in the castle that will fit her and you will force her, however strenuously you must insist—" he took another deep breath and tried to sound imposing "—to sit through an entire meal with me. I have often felt I would die of boredom, so it might be dangerous as well."

The two faces in front of him froze. Mistress Kay's broke first. Tilting her head, she whispered, "Sire?"

Philip walked to the door. "I understand this punishment might be considered more dire than some, but I did make a promise to Lady Coralee." He placed his hand on the door handle, but the question he wanted to avoid came before he could open it.

"But, Your Majesty," Mistress Kay cleared her throat, "wouldn't it be deceitful for the girl to dress above her station? She hasn't been trained as a noble. She wouldn't know how to act properly at a dinner with a king. Do you wish to mock her?"

Philip turned to face her. "We may live in the Noble Kingdom and aspire to magnify our stations in life, but my sister and I have been discussing the competence and natural nobility of the common people. I would like to hear Tierni's opinion of the matter. Mocking her would only lessen my nobility. I would never mock her." He could barely keep himself from wincing at the last part.

Could I sound more desperate to dine with a servant? he berated himself.

He yanked the door open with more force than he had planned. "Her punishment will take place tomorrow night and she must perform it alone," he announced loudly for the benefit of the guards as well.

The two women mumbled agreement, dipped curtsies, and scurried from the room. Tierni halted in front of Philip. She lifted her chin to meet his eyes for a moment—a moment Philip drank in—before Mistress Kay jerked her arm to pull her into the hallway.

Now the only problem would be making sure Philip could act like a king with those eyes on him over dinner.

14

TAKING FLIGHT

Hiro slipped into Rakgar's lair while the sky was still gray and a handful of stars continued to wink down at him. He didn't want to dodge requests from Tog or Prak to join him. Plus, he hadn't slept well. He thought about Priya for most of the night. Where she would be going? Would she remain in the Rock Clouds? Should he say goodbye to her? What would he even have to say? He hadn't come up with any answers.

Even at this early hour, Rakgar slept in the large lair that was meant for him to meet with the other dragons. Hiro questioned whether he bothered to sleep in another lair anywhere else. He always wanted to be easily accessible to the ruck.

Hiro lingered briefly to watch him sleep, reflecting on how this dragon had practically helped his sires raise him. He knew Rakgar would always do what he believed to be best for the ruck. He would protect other dragons to his own detriment, Hiro was sure. *The only reason he had made poor decisions of late must be because of that demon faerie, Skorkot.*

He searched the cave around him for the faerie. *No, he thought to himself, she must be sleeping in Rakgar's lair. That's why Rakgar is out here. Caring for and worrying about others will be that dan's downfall.*

Hiro crept closer to wake the mighty gray dragon, but before he could whisper a word Rakgar leapt into the air, knocked Hiro to the ground, and stood atop him with a raised claw.

"Rakgar!" Hiro struggled to speak with Rakgar pressing the air from his lungs. "I've come for the human!" Rakgar's eyes burned. If he had looked any angrier, fire might have erupted from them. Rakgar placed a claw on Hiro's neck and pressed. "Rakgar," Hiro clawed at his leader's leg, "it's morning. I came as you ordered. Please!"

The terrifying dragon finally stepped from Hiro, but his eyes still burned with rage. "Yes," Rakgar nodded, "the human must leave."

Hiro nodded and coughed as he clambered to his feet. While he recovered, Rakgar stepped to the crevice in the wall that led to Priya's lair. He wedged his head and neck through the gap, but nothing more than a claw would fit through after that.

He yelled to Priya and the sound echoed through the cavern. When she answered, Hiro could hear anxiety in her voice. While Hiro and Rakgar waited for the woman to appear, Rakgar stepped close to Hiro.

"Don't trust her," he whispered. "I know you feel honor-bound to help her, but you must remember that she is human. She will lie and manipulate you. Return her to the surface and be rid of her."

The advice sounded much like Priya's. The two dragons agreed on more than either of them would admit. Before Hiro could question Rakgar, Anna scrambled from the opening of Priya's lair.

She took measured steps toward Hiro while Rakgar hissed at her. Hiro forced himself to stay seated and allow her to come to him. She walked carefully with her chin high until she stood next to Hiro.

"Are you unharmed?" Hiro asked.

She simply nodded.

Rakgar stalked to his previous sleeping position. "Get her out of here before I change my mind," he growled.

Hiro turned to lope from the cave with Princess Anna following at his side. Once they stepped onto the rocky slopes of the Inner Mountain, Hiro scooped her into his claw.

Bounding into the sky, he muttered, "Let's get you out of here."

Anna clung to his leg but tried to keep her voice low as she asked, "Aren't you worried that others will see you carrying me?"

"I don't care," he growled. His heart contracted as he thought about getting the woman away from the dangers in the Rock Clouds. But the next moment it softened again, so he assumed it was because he had previously been thinking about Priya.

Springtime made the early morning air warm and pleasant. They flew toward the Black Forest until all signs of night fled. Anna lay quietly curled in a ball in Hiro's claw. He didn't dare bother her. She most likely hadn't slept well either. His suspicion was confirmed when she lolled, but quickly recovered her position.

"We have to stop for your bag," he told her after the third time she slipped. "We'll rest there."

"Anywhere is better than in that cave." He felt her shiver violently. "For the most part, I just sat in the dark by myself. When that green dragon appeared, she just glared at me. She never said a word. She just…stared. I suppose it was better than staying with the big gray one. Rakgar?"

Hiro rolled his shoulder. "I'm not sure which of them is more dangerous."

Hiro must have pressed his wings harder than ever because Centaur River came into view not long after the sun had passed its zenith. The pair spotted the large boulder jutting over the water to mark where they hid Anna's bag of supplies.

As they tumbled to the ground Anna could hold on no longer. Her grip on Hiro's leg loosened and sent her sprawling on her belly to the forest floor before the dragon landed. She lay in silence, her feet resting on some mossy new growth. Hiro listened for danger, but since they weren't in the Black Forest yet, he didn't expect anything.

Once Hiro began to move, Anna waved a hand from where she'd landed, laying on top of a large branch. "I'll get my bag later," she mumbled into the dirt.

"You won't be very comfortable there," Hiro said, walking over to a tree surrounded by green shoots coming up from the forest floor.

Anna half-opened one eye. With a groan, she hoisted herself onto her hands and knees and crawled to follow him. Her once resplendent gown and cloak, now coated in dust and dirt, dragged across the greenery.

She laid her head on Hiro's front claw, curling her back against his soft underbelly, a position to which the two of them had become accustomed. Hiro curled his leathery wing over her. The last thing he remembered before he fell asleep was both of them heaving a sigh together.

15

TRIFLING TASTES

"Sire," Ruther's voice made Philip realize he was pacing again. He stopped and turned to his servant. "Is there anything I can get you? Some wine, perhaps?"

"No, thank you, Ruther." He could barely keep himself from picking up his foot again. He didn't want any wine, even the watered-down version he had at meals. He wanted a clear head tonight. But even still, he motioned for his servant to come closer. "I came too early, didn't I? I've made everyone uncomfortable."

Ruther leaned his head closer to the king. "They certainly weren't expecting you now, Sire. Tradition dictates that you arrive last." The tall servant, brother of Philip's regular servant, didn't quite come up to Philip's nose. Ruther shrugged his shoulders, "But you're here now. I think they'll understand your nerves when she arrives."

Ruther had used the extra time to make sure everything was ready for Philip's dinner with Tierni. He shifted the flowers in the centerpiece. He had a glass exchanged that he announced wasn't sturdy enough. Philip appreciated all his servants' knowledge and sensitivity.

When the great double doors swung open, Philip jerked his head around so fast he felt a twinge of pain at the base of his skull. When Torgon walked through, he reached around to rub the sore spot. "Oh, it's you," he said.

Torgon's face scrunched when he saw the young king. "Sorry to disappoint," he said with a questioning grin. "Who were you expecting?"

Philip's hand slid from his neck and he shrugged. "I invited someone to dinner."

Torgon stopped himself from pulling his own chair out. Normally, if Anna didn't show up (and she rarely did these days), the two young men didn't stand on ceremony and tucked themselves in as soon as they both arrived. Now Torgon stood behind his chair, formally folding both of his hands to one side of his hips. His eyebrows rose almost to meet his hairline. "Did you, now?" Philip rolled his eyes, but Torgon continued. "Who is she? The older blonde? The younger redhead?"

Philip shook his head. "None of those."

"None?" Torgon's eyes lit up. "Then where did you meet her? Who is she? What's her name?"

"Her name is—"

Philip was interrupted by the great double doors swinging open again. He drew in a sharp breath when she appeared. She wore a gown of deep red with pleated fabric that crossed her chest and stretched up to the edge of her shoulder. Her hair, instead of being pulled tightly to the back of her head as it had been when they met, tumbled in loose ringlets to brush her shoulders. Philip tried to banish the image of her soft shoulder against his cheek. She wore no jewelry or gilding on her gown, but her blue eyes sparkled and Philip thought her lovely face the only jewel she need ever wear. He opened his mouth to speak.

"Tierni!" Torgon shouted before Philip could say a word. "What are you doing here? Why are you wearing that? What are you thinking?" He marched over to her and grabbed her arm, wrenching her toward the door.

Philip bristled at his best friend's action, then realized. "You know her?"

Tierni deftly twisted her arm free of Torgon's. In the back of Philip's mind, he took note that Torgon was strong and well-trained, but this diminutive young woman had freed herself from his grasp easier than plucking a grape.

"I was invited by the king," she snapped back at Torgon. She stared him in the eye without fear. "I was instructed to wear this."

Philip directed his attention to Torgon. "How do you know her?"

"This is who you invited?" Torgon spun on him as if he'd done something wrong. "Why didn't you tell me?"

Philip threw his hands up in defense as Torgon advanced on him. "I didn't know I required your permission!" Had Torgon seen her in the halls? Had he noticed her as a servant? Did he know her from his earlier years in the army?

"Why did you invite her? Her? All the noble women and courtiers you've met, and you invite her?" Torgon demanded, continuing his aggressive advance so far that the guards at the door gripped their sword hilts.

Philip flashed a palm at the guards to halt them. "Torgon," Philip spoke slowly and clearly, "how do you know her?"

Torgon straightened his back and tugged at his tunic to compose himself. He glanced back at Tierni, who crossed her arms at her chest and narrowed dangerous eyes at him.

Turning back to Philip, Torgon set his lips so hard in anger that they almost disappeared. "She's my sister."

Philip swallowed. He opened his mouth but nothing came out. His mind had gone blank.

Torgon spun back to Tierni. "And she's leaving this instant," he growled.

He started to grab her arm again, but she swung it away and planted it on her hip. "I'm afraid not," she thrust her chin at him. "I'm here as a punishment and I intend to be held accountable."

Torgon's face twisted. "Punishment?"

"Uh," Philip's mouth hung agape. "Something of a poor excuse," he mumbled apologetically to Torgon, "I can explain later."

Torgon jabbed a finger in Philip's direction. "And you will, but," he spun on Tierni, "you're not staying here. It's not your place."

Tierni jutted her chin toward her brother again. "I was ordered by the king. Do you think yourself above the king?"

Silence throbbed through the large dining room. Philip held his breath along with the servants, the guards, and Ruther. What could he possibly say if Torgon answered "Yes"?

Torgon's head dipped and he glanced at Philip through lowered eyes. "No." When he whispered the word, Philip heard Ruther exhale. "But," Torgon continued and Philip suppressed the urge to grind his teeth, "I do feel equal to any man involved with my sister." Torgon's head lifted and he stared Philip in the eye. "I'm sorry, Philip, but as the head of my household I must insist on some time to consider the situation before I can allow any involvement between the two of you."

"That's perfectly understandable," Philip nodded. Glancing to Tierni, he pleaded with his eyes for her to understand as well. However, dropping her hands to her sides, she stormed out of the room.

Philip turned his attention back to Torgon, although his mind lingered on the memory of Tierni's gown whipping around the corner. "Torgon," he pleaded, "if I had known…"

"I know," Torgon held up a hand to forestall the apology, "but I think I'll take my meal elsewhere tonight."

Once he left the room, Philip flopped into his chair. Putting his hands over his face, he groaned.

———

Hiro awoke to the sound of snuffling in the dirt behind him. Keeping his eyes closed, he heard breathing, almost snorting. A scrape of what sounded like bone on wood. Vegetation tearing from the earth and…chomping. A heartbeat. Just one. But a scent like nothing he'd ever experienced. It smelled…like moonlight.

He couldn't explain it. He couldn't place it. He knew it wasn't a danger, but curiosity got the better of him.

Careful not to move his claws and startle Anna, Hiro lifted his head from the ground to snake it around and face the creature. Moonlight glimmered from a long silvery mane and tail that brushed the ground. A radiant white coat magnified the light around it. Night bugs and flickers of dust shadow spun the air as if to draw the focus of every living thing around it. Four glistening hooves and a single twisted horn shimmered like thousands of majikally embellished snork trails. It seemed as though a shake of its head might call the stars from the sky above to shine down around it.

Hiro felt Anna sit up. She didn't make a sound as she peered over Hiro's shoulder, but she gasped when she saw it too.

"A unicorn," she whispered. "They *do* exist!"

"Of course they do," Hiro whispered back. He had seen memories of unicorns from other dragons in the ruck, but the sightings were extremely rare.

"Well, how would I know?" she shrunk back a little. "Faeries say that they'll only appear to dragons."

Hiro shrugged, "Then how would *they* know?"

"Why would they only appear to dragons?" Anna mused. "Dragons are such dangerous and ferocious creatures. Wouldn't a dragon eat a unicorn?"

Both the unicorn and the dragon turned to look at her. Anna's eyes widened. "A dragon would never dare eat a unicorn," Hiro rumbled low. "What good would ever come from harming something so pure and majikal?"

The unicorn dipped its head back to the sparse undergrowth.

Anna pursed her lips, "I thought you would eat anything with a heartbeat."

Hiro tilted his head to glance at her then shifted it back to the unicorn. "We don't eat absolutely everything that crosses our path. I would never eat a—" he glanced again to see Anna watching him, "unicorn."

"Have you ever eaten a faerie?"

"No, but there are several that I might try to eat."

Hiro stretched his neck over to the unicorn. It stood idly chomping at the shoots in its mouth. Hiro reached a claw toward it. He heard Anna's breath catch moments before the shimmering creature nuzzled its snout into the pad of his claw. He stroked two talons through the thick, glistening mane before the creature bent its neck to get another mouthful of spring grass.

Anna exhaled as Hiro retracted his claw. The two of them gazed at the resplendent beast. Anna draped herself across Hiro's neck. "Would you ever eat a centaur?"

"Of course not," he answered, "they're our allies."

Anna remained silent for a moment. "What about another dragon?"

"Now that would be murder." The unicorn snuffled behind them, stepping further into the forest.

"Not a dragon from your ruck," she defended her theory.

"Even to hunt or attack a dragon from another ruck would be criminal. Would you hunt another human? Even a human from a different kingdom?"

"What about the flightless type?"

"All humans are flightless."

"No, I meant dragons."

Hiro turned to face her. Now she was getting to the heart of it. "What are you asking?"

"Would you ever hunt or eat one of those flightless dragons?" she clarified.

"The ones that live in the marshes at the south end of Centaur River?" She nodded. Hiro scrunched up his face. "I'm not sure," he answered honestly. "If I were extremely hungry, maybe. But a dragon is a dragon, even the flightless, non-intelligent type."

"Wait," Anna stood up straight, spooking the unicorn a few steps away, "the flightless dragons can't speak?"

"We call them 'worms,'" Hiro shook his head, "and no, the gift of speech has not spread among them."

Anna's head tipped. "So, is it intelligence that determines your attitude toward creatures?"

He shook his head at her. "Unicorns don't speak either."

She settled onto the ground, leaning her back against Hiro. "You don't make any sense."

Hiro settled himself around her. "It's simple. I've heard that unicorns taste awful," he said with a smile. The unicorn tossed its head, shook its mane, and turned its back on them.

16

A REQUEST

"I've made a mess of things," Philip muttered. He stared into the marble eyes of his father.

"It can't be all that bad," said a voice from behind him. The voice belonged to Tommak. Probably the only man in Kingstor Noble to match Philip in height, Tommak stood to one side, examining a metal bust which floated above the floor at eye level and depicted another of Philip's ancestors.

Philip couldn't take his eyes away from his father's likeness. "He lived his entire life in peace. No wars. No rogue dragons threatening his kingdom. No faeries bullying him into wars. As soon as he departs, I botch it all for him."

He felt Tommak step up behind him. "Your father would be proud of the king you have become."

"The faeries don't respect me," he grumbled, feeling like the young child that had once fallen from his horse. It wasn't a terrible fall, but Tommak had been there with a kind word and a piece of candy. "I feel I have to struggle to gain the respect of my own generals and officers. A crazy, blood-thirsty dragon is running around my kingdom intent on murdering me and…my best friend is avoiding me."

"The faeries don't respect anyone but themselves," Tommak countered. "You are, in fact, gaining the respect of your men, even though the stubborn old trolls among them will always oppose you. And the dragon's menace could have happened to anyone."

"You say nothing of Torgon."

Tommak sighed. "That is a matter of the heart. When you figure that one out, let the rest of us know."

Philip grinned when he glanced back and saw the general's smile. "I probably should have made you Royal General."

Tommak cast his eyes to the statue of the late king. "Your father might have."

At this response, Philip turned completely to face Tommak, the smile melting from his face. "You think I should have." It was not a question. No one in their right mind would turn down the position. It was the highest honor in the kingdom.

Tommak turned his ever-gentle eyes to Philip. "I did not say that." He took a deep breath and looked again at the statue with fondness. "Your father might have chosen me for my loyalty and long experience. But you," he placed one hand on Philip's shoulder, "you needed more than a Royal General."

Philip's gaze dropped to the ground. "And now I've ruined that too."

Tommak gently shook his shoulder. "Only if you give up on it."

Before Philip could answer, a side door to the Hall of Kings flew open. Boots beat across the floor until Torgon swung around a double-sided portrait of an entire royal family rotating in the center of the hall. Philip's stomach roiled. The last time he had felt like this was when he made his first appearance performing audiences in his father's stead. He remembered the sweaty palms and nausea well.

"Tommak," Torgon nodded to the general. "Your Majesty," he indicated Philip with a nod of his head.

"Royal General," Tommak responded before Torgon could say anything, "I was just excusing myself." He faced Philip with a salute. "Your Majesty."

Tommak scurried away before Philip could even nod in his direction, and the two young men were left standing together in the shadows of the kings.

"Philip," Torgon stood up straight with his hands clasped in front of him. "I'm sorry I didn't return sooner, but I think I've found a temporary solution to our problem."

Philip's eyebrows pinched together, thinking only of Tierni. "What problem is that?"

"Captain Murzod," Torgon said. His matter-of-fact attitude made Philip question if his best friend actually had been avoiding him. When he nodded with understanding, Torgon continued. "I've found another faerie who has a good idea of the spells Kradik might use to travel quickly. Although he's not willing to travel with us, he said he would be willing to use his majik to get us to the halfway point much faster."

"Us?" Philip asked.

"The men I've chosen and myself," Torgon said.

Philip nodded. "When will you leave?"

Torgon clasped his hands behind his back. "Within the hour."

Philip nodded again, hoping the movement would hide the teeth he couldn't unclench. "Very well," he finally answered. "I'll see your group off shortly."

Torgon jerked his head and spun on his heel. But before he had gone two paces, he stopped. Slowly he turned back to face Philip. "You're being very good about this, Philip. Much better than I am, I'm afraid. And I'm sorry," Torgon continued, lowering his voice. "I don't blame you for anything. It's just—" he scrubbed his hand through his hair, a sure sign of his frustration. "I just don't know what to do. I mean, it's not like you're not a good guy—you're like my own brother! But she's my sister. My only sister. And she's so young—I never thought to even consider you and—well, I couldn't, could I?" He took a long, deep breath. "I am still your friend and I want to prove it, so I'll give you two things."

Intrigued, Philip tipped his head quizzically but said nothing. "First," Torgon continued, "a promise. I promise that when I return, I will give you an answer as to my feelings about your involvement with my sister. And second..." Torgon paused. His scrunched his face to one side. He cleared his throat, ran his fingers through his hair again, scratched his neck, then crossed his arms in front of his chest. Tightening his lips before he spoke, he met Philip's eyes. "Her name is Josie." Then his finger swung out and came within hairs of the king's nose. "And, so help me, if you tease me about her, I'll beat you with your own crown."

With that, Philip's best friend raced from the room before either of them could say *treason*.

———

A large boulder jutted from the tree canopy beneath them. Curved on one side and flat on the other, it looked like a giant dagger slicing through the greenery. Almost at its peak for the day, the sun shined on the pair, lending warmth and comfort. Hiro drifted on a wind current taking him south of the massive rock as Anna called out to him.

"Hiro!" He glanced down at her, but she stared at the boulder as if it signified something. "I need to ask you a favor."

"Since when do you ask?" he chuckled.

"This is serious," she held no levity in her voice, "and it could potentially be dangerous."

"Just being in your presence is dangerous…and disgusting," he answered with a grin. When she didn't say any more, he rolled his shoulder and looked down at her again. "Do I need to land to hear this favor?"

"Yes." Her eyes never left the rock formation, then she pointed to it. "Over there."

Hiro's eyes made a wide arc back into his head at the lack of information, but he tilted his wings to spiral down next to the large, pointed boulder. He dipped into the canopy of leaves. The green side of the leaves faced the sun while the gold side faced the ground, and the leaves of the Golden firs sparkled overhead when they touched down. Dapples of shimmering sunlight speckled the hytocomp beneath their feet.

"Lovely area," Hiro inspected the forest around them, "but would you mind telling me why we're down here and not flying you home right now?"

Anna searched the trees as well, but said nothing. Turning in circles, she almost looked lost until she suddenly sprinted south. "This way!" she yelled over her shoulder.

Her little legs had nothing on Hiro, so he loped after her, taking his time. As they moved along, Hiro began to wonder if Anna would ever explain their purpose here. Her legs moved swifter than he'd ever seen them go. She would falter only slightly, get her bearings, and bound into the trees again. He tried to question her, but she would silence him with a wave and continue to run.

When she finally stopped, her face was flushed, her hairline was wet, and her breath came in gasps. Hiro stepped next to her as she leaned over, hands on her knees, to catch her breath. "Is this the favor? To watch you run through the forest? Because you don't have to ask me to do that. I'm always willing."

She shook her head, her chest heaving as she lifted a finger to point into the trees. "Shampy."

Hiro spun. The scales on his claw hadn't yet grown back from the spot where the twisted little faerie shaman had tortured him. "What? Where?" His eyes searched the trees.

As he focused further in, he could see a small hut made of green stone. The golden leaves camouflaged the little building with shimmering light. The thatched roof reflected the same golden branches overhead.

"How did you find my summer home, dragon?"

The gravelly voice came from above and behind him. Hiro tripped over his tail and thumped Anna to the ground with it before he could find the little faerie named Shampy.

"As graceful as ever, I see," she said, once he faced her. She crouched on a branch overlooking the two. Having traded her dirty blue cloth for a faded red one hadn't improved her appearance. The silvery hair on one side of her head was divided into three sections, braided, and twisted up toward the sky, like three dragon horns. The snake tattoo on the other side didn't shine as it had when they'd met before, but Hiro assumed it would only do that in dim light.

"Your summer home?" Hiro growled at her and stared down at Anna as she picked herself from the mossy ground. "What are we doing here? Is this your favor?"

"Shampy," Anna addressed the withered old faerie, "another shaman told me where to find you."

"What shaman?" Hiro hissed.

"Never you mind," she shot back at him. "I have to ask you something," she said to the faerie.

"Ask me something?" Shampy sprang from the branch to the ground. Although she had been more than a dragon's length from the ground, she landed lightly on her feet without the use of her wings. She stood to her full, yet stooped, height and punched her fists on her hips. "Favors? Incantations? Fortunes? Spells?" Her wrinkled translucent skin shook as she stamped her feet. "Help me with this!" she wailed in a high pitch. "Teach me that!" she screamed low. "I love him! I don't love her! My brother, mother, sister, son! My horse won't run! My cat won't mew! I need majik! They need majik! We need majik! I can't do it without majik! I need you! He needs you! She needs you! Help me! Help me! Help me! Don't you know I come here to get away from all of that?"

"I need to speak to the dead!" Anna shouted abruptly.

Shampy ceased her tirade. Her hands swung to her sides. Her eyes narrowed. "You must be desperate to ask this."

Anna nodded.

"And let me guess," Shampy stood still. More still than Hiro had ever seen her. "You have nothing to pay for this service, and I use the term 'service' very loosely because what you ask…is actually more…of a curse."

"I'll give you whatever I can as well as ingredients for the majik, but I have nothing with me right now. I'll have to bring you something at a later time or maybe…"

Anna's voice drifted off as Shampy lifted one gnarled hand. "Peace." She lowered her hand and shook her head. "Do you even understand what you're asking?"

Hiro's eyes had been bouncing between the two. Now he snaked his head around to position it between the two of them. "Do you?" he asked Anna.

"Yes," she whispered into his eyes. She peeked around him and told the old woman in a firmer voice, "Yes, I do."

Shampy grinned, without lips a sickening smile to see, and waves of wrinkled muscle on her face finished the effect. "You might know the possible consequences, but you have no idea the cost." The old faerie opened her wings. "Come," she motioned toward the hut as she drifted toward it, "we shall see if I can dissuade you."

On the opposite side of the little building they found a couple of stumps, the insides of them scooped out and smoothed over. Anna slipped comfortably into one. The remnants of a fire sputtered between the chairs. With amazing deftness for one so old, Shampy hefted a couple of trimmed branches from a nearby pile.

"Dragon," Shampy said, after placing the logs in front of them within the burnt remains, "I wouldn't insult you by trying to light a fire in front of you. While you do that, I'll get us some refreshment. This is, after all, my holiday."

As Shampy shuffled into the hut, Hiro spit some fire on the logs. They crackled with welcome and, though they were further south now and the springtime should have warmed them, the heat from the fire was comforting.

Shampy scuffled back from the hut carrying two small cups of a bright blue liquid and a green sprig as long as her forearm. Around her waist was a braided rope that held a small leather satchel. She handed one of the cups to

Anna, then turned and offered the sprig to Hiro. "I was able to find some mint in my stores. Just enough for some refreshment."

Hiro curled on the ground next to Anna's seat. He wrapped his tongue around a few of the green leaves. They melted inside his mouth, but the mesmerizing flavor wasn't enough to distract him from the conversation going on in front of him.

"Now," Shampy said as she sighed, leaning back in her stump, "so many questions. Where do I start?"

Anna stared silently into her drink.

"Alright," Shampy nodded, then took a swig from her cup. Her eyes never left the princess. She took a deep breath. "Whom do you wish to contact in The World of Souls?"

Anna closed her eyes. "My father." When Anna met Shampy's eyes again, one of the little witch's white eyebrows lifted. "King Paudie of the Noble Kingdom," Anna clarified.

"He's not the king anymore," Shampy said. "I'll need his base name."

"Paudie ido Patrick and Arllyl feira Prince and King of the Noble Kingdom."

Shampy shrugged. "I guess that will have to do." She shifted in her seat and thrust her hand into the bag at her side. "Let me start by saying, I don't know if I'm even strong enough for the spell. It usually takes a circle of at least three shaman to perform the majik, not to mention the others to…" she pulled her hand out of her bag, but kept it in a fist, holding something. "Well, let's just say it's not a one-shaman spell!"

"I know you can do it," Anna almost whispered.

Shampy barked a laugh. "Your faith in my skills aside, you need to know what you're asking." She mumbled in faerie tongue into her fist, then cast the contents into the fire.

Sparks jumped into the air. The flames danced and twisted, then turned a brilliant blue. Images floated in the flame. The ancient faerie drank from her cup, gargled the gulp, then swallowed it and cleared her throat. Her eyes shone as her lids lifted higher.

"The World of Souls is protected from our world for good reason," the shaman growled. "Imagine if we could commune with the souls of the dead whenever we desired. Friendships and bonds would continue as if never having been parted." Two people danced out of the flames, hand-in-hand, one light, one dark. "New bonds would develop." Several new couples of all shapes and sizes danced and mixed in large groups. "Meeting someone's family would include ancient relatives, none of which seem to be older than the peak of their lives." As she said that a young man stood before them being introduced to a young woman by another young woman. They conversed silently for a moment, then, amidst tears, he walked away arm-in-arm with the second young woman.

"With those bonds would come truth. Truth can be the great destroyer." Another man made of dark light appeared and whispered in a young woman's ear. She screamed a silent echo and ran away from him. "Not a single aspect of one's life can be hidden among the dead. Murderers, liars, thieves, desecrators, all exposed." Several dark shapes of men and women contorted around those made of light. "All dwell in The World of Souls alongside lovers, parents, and victims. Not only could we get many answers, but we could get too many." A dark woman followed a light woman before them, showing the light woman tossing in her sleep as the dark woman whispered in her ear.

"But that isn't the worst of what you ask." Shampy snapped her fingers and the fire split in two. "When a soul moves between our two worlds," a single flame leapt from one side of the blue fire to the other, "it leaves both worlds vulnerable. Whether the tear is made in death or by a visiting soul, there is always a rend between the two worlds." The single leaping flame left a long trail of fire behind it. "Good and evil may pass back and forth to influence, shift, and even force the ways of both worlds." Dark souls poured through the gap of flame. "The living could be plagued by the dead."

"However," Shampy's voice continued, "dragon souls are the guardians of the gateway between the two worlds." Several dragon shapes, both light and dark, sprang up between the two sides of the fire. "It is said that the dragons have taken it upon themselves to safeguard the passage of souls. I've personally never known a dragon to be so selfless—," Hiro growled at her, "but all the same, from what we know of The World of Souls, it seems to be true."

Anna, who had watched the performance unblinking, now looked up at Shampy as the fire returned to normal. "What does it mean? In order to summon a soul, we must force our way past the souls of dragons?"

"Tartaku would never allow it," Hiro said.

"Not force our way," Shampy shook her head, settling back. "There's no way to force past the soul of a dragon. No."

"Then what?" Anna sat forward, spreading her hands. "You can't tell me it's impossible, because I know that it is possible. Whether done by your majik or not, I know it is possible. What will it take? What must I do?"

Shampy drained her cup, belched out loud, then pointed a dirty fingernail at Hiro. "The only way to open the gateway between the worlds and summon the dead…" she dropped her finger and grinned, "is through the death of a dragon."

Anna's jaw plummeted. "No," she shook her head. "There has to be another way."

"Only the soul of a dragon will create a space amidst the other dragon souls in the gateway long enough for us to summon those you need to commune with." She grinned again. "A dragon must die.

"As for payment, that really is moot," Shampy said, glaring into her empty cup. "I don't even know if the majik will work with only me to perform the task, but I will say I consider the death of a dragon payment enough. The most difficult part will be convincing a dragon to die so you can speak with your dead father. Oh," she sat up straighter, "I can't promise how much time you will have with him either. Maybe minutes, maybe only seconds, there's no way to know."

"Is this the favor?" Hiro rounded on Anna. "Are you asking me to die for you so you can speak with your father for a few seconds?"

"Of course not," Anna shot back at him. "I would never ask that of you! I only wanted you to come with me to see her. I'm terrified to be alone with her!"

The pair of them looked over at the old shaman as she crossed her leg over her knee to scratch the bottom of her foot, exposing everything beneath the faded cloth she wore.

As Hiro muttered something about humans not being the only disgusting creature, Anna jumped to her feet. "The death of a dragon!" she proclaimed.

Hiro shook his head. "Not something to look forward to."

"No, no, no," Anna shook her head at him then turned to Shampy. "Can it be any dragon?"

Shampy narrowed an eye at her. "Yes, of course."

"I'm not going to ask anyone to die for—" Hiro started, but Anna cut him off.

"Any dragon at all?" she asked the old woman. "Even, say, an unintelligent one?"

Hiro's eyebrows dropped. "What are you saying?"

Shampy sighed, the thrill of the task erased from her face. "Yes, I suppose an unintelligent one would work just as well."

"Ha!" Anna shouted.

"A worm?" Hiro asked.

"Of course!" Anna looked up at him. "You said yourself that you think of flightless dragons as little more than animals. But they are still dragons! It would be like sacrificing a cow or a lion to serve our purpose."

"I suppose," Hiro hemmed.

"You must bring it to me alive," Shampy stood. "It cannot die a moment sooner than the spell is cast."

"You'll do it, then?" Anna asked her.

Shampy walked in a small circle. When she faced Anna again, she nodded. "I'll do it. On the condition that I can keep the dragon from turning to ash and harvest it myself after the spell. That should be more than enough payment and compensation of ingredients."

"Hiro," Anna said, then turned her small face up to his. "Will you do it? Will you help me?"

He rumbled in the back of his throat. "I don't like it, Anna. Not with an intelligent dragon or a worm. I don't like it."

"Please, Hiro." She placed her hands on his shoulder. "Please, this is important."

He rolled his other shoulder, shook his head, thumped his tail, and rolled his shoulder again. Looking back into her longing eyes, he said, "Of course, I'll help you."

17

KEELED

It took them two days to fly to the closest herd of flightless dragons in the south. The beasts didn't even realize Hiro and Anna were there before they snatched a young orange dragon, barely more than a fledgling, from under the unobservant noses of its sires. Hiro could easily handle the little worm and carried it back to Shampy's summer home unimpeded.

When he pinned it to the ground with his claws in front of her hut, Shampy crossed her arms at her chest. "Didn't go for a big one, did you? No, I suppose that would be too much work for you, wouldn't it?" She walked around the dragon, running her hand over its legs and occasionally tapping it with her foot.

"Why do you look it over like a horse master inspecting a prize stallion?" Anna asked. "I thought you said it didn't matter what kind of dragon we used."

"It doesn't," Shampy said, continuing to walk the length of the dragon. When she reached its head, she pulled a handful of something from the satchel at her waist. "I just want to know exactly what I'm getting." She jerked her chin as if satisfied, stepped in front of the small dragon's head, opened her hand, and blew a puff of white powder in its face. The dragon fell still.

Hiro knew the use of that powder intimately. That was the same powder used to imprison him at Kingstor Noble. He jerked away from the faerie, and the now-unconscious dragon, as she dusted off her hands.

"That would have been helpful in the capture," Anna pointed out.

"And I would've offered it, if I'd had it at the time," Shampy said, while she turned and stoked the fire behind her. "But I had to contact an acquaintance of mine to request its use. No thanks to you two, I now owe a romantic dinner to an old beau—Skyttel-fits, that will be a travesty!"

Anna and Hiro settled themselves on the opposite side of the fire from Shampy. It seemed she'd brought half of the interior of her home outside. Several green banners with silver markings hung from branches surrounding the area. They watched her build totems of rocks and twigs and moss that dotted the ground. Dried herbs hung in bunches tied to tree trunks and scattered in circles around the totems. Around the fire she laid several dishes of varying sizes and colors. Each contained a different specimen.

Hiro tried to content himself by lying on the ground behind Anna. Anna asked if she could help the old faerie, but got a hearty laugh in response. After a while she sat down on the ground next to Hiro and they tried to guess quietly what things were in the different dishes and what they might be used for.

Shampy paused in her work to give Anna a plate of colorful leaves and dark purple berries. "What am I supposed to do with them?" Anna asked, poking at the berries. "Do I sprinkle them somewhere or stomp them or something?"

"No," Shampy bent over, making her jowls fall forward, "you eat them. That's what one usually does when offered food." She had also brought a plate for herself and sat in one of the chairs to eat.

"Once the incantation begins, you can't interrupt me," she told them with purple juice dripping down her chin. "The dragon will wake while I kill it, but the incantation will hold it still. Say nothing. Do nothing. Don't even breathe, if you can help it, until Paudie appears. Then you can speak to him freely until he disappears."

Shampy finished eating and returned to her preparations. When she began pouring a foul-smelling liquid on the totems, Hiro nudged Anna with his snout. "Do you want me to stay for this?" he asked. "I can slip away so you can have a private conversation with your father."

"No," Anna shook her head and put her plate on the ground. "Shampy will hear everything anyway. I would prefer you to stay with me."

"Besides," Shampy shouted to them from the other side of the sleeping dragon, "you have to be here to make the majik stronger. It might end the incantation sooner if you leave."

Hiro laid his head on his claws. "I guess I'll stay, then."

Soon after this conversation, the old woman rubbed a white grease over her entire body then dipped her hands in the foul-stenched stuff dripping from the totems. The grease helped conceal her muscles and tendons, almost making her skin seem opaque. Hiro wondered briefly why the faeries didn't try to dye their skin to make it opaque. He almost asked this question before the grease turned transparent as well.

Anna watched in shock. She turned to Hiro and whispered, "This must also be part of the curse. I wonder how her tattoo stays visible."

Shampy stood on the opposite side of the fire from them. "Are you ready?" she asked. When they both nodded, she grinned. "And the tattoo was there before the curse took hold. I have several others that you can't see because they were applied afterward."

She lifted her hands into the air and began chanting. As she chanted, Hiro caught snippets of words and phrases that he understood from Faerie Tongue. She repeated "into the fire" several times before she put her hands in the fire and the flames licked and stuck to them. When her hands caught fire, the totems caught fire as well. With the sun falling behind the trees, the small fires lit the area surrounding them. Shadows danced as the old shaman swayed, tossing the coordinated fires to and fro. Hiro heard Paudie's base name twice.

She chanted again (something about "into the fire" and "come from the flame"), lifting each ingredient from the dishes surrounding the fire and throwing them in. Hiro caught the names of some of them in Faerie Tongue. *Beetle tongues? What is that supposed to be for? Hytocomp? Doesn't that have water? Wouldn't it douse the fire?* But the fire grew.

Shampy's hands continued to burn, but Hiro noticed that wherever she had smeared the white grease, the fire didn't spread to that part of her body. And the flames on her hands didn't burn, but only licked them over the surface.

After all the ingredients had been added, Shampy chanted louder. Stronger. There was no hint of the gravelly, frail voice of the faerie shaman they had come to know. She stood up straight, her hands burning over her head. Her voice screamed into the sky.

A knife flew into her hand. Hiro had no idea where it had come from. The edges of the long dagger shimmered with majikal light. A wind swept through the trees, fully fluttering the flags on the branches, and they didn't fall. Shampy's chanting grew louder as she turned to face the unconscious dragon on the ground behind her. All the fires surrounding them grew. The little totems burned bright and high enough to light the herbs tied halfway up the tree trunks. With a screech, Shampy plunged the dagger into the dragon's neck and dragged it down the length of its body.

The dragon's eyes flew open. It wriggled as if to stand, but it couldn't. Its jaw worked and its tongue lashed. Open, close, open, close. It blinked a few times and its entire body shuttered. It shuddered and shook as the old shaman continued screaming her chant, over and over. The dragon convulsed to the rhythm of the words. With one more loud bellow, Shampy's incantation ceased. The dragon stilled. Its chest didn't rise and fall. Its eyes glazed over and remained open.

Shampy shook her head. A small movement, but Hiro caught it. Anna turned to face Hiro. The obvious question on her face. Did it work?

The flags in the trees now fluttered naturally with a soft breeze. The fires settled to a gentle crackling. The entire clearing in front of the little hut quieted.

"Anna." All three of them spun at the sound of a man's voice. He stepped out from behind Shampy's hut. He was tall and handsome, with dark hair and a strong jaw.

"Father?" Anna whispered.

The man stepped toward her. As Hiro watched he was reminded of the time not long ago that a woman had appeared to him, telling him to go to his friend. Having listened to her, he was able to save Tog from death. This man made no sound as he stepped across the ground and left no footprints behind him, as had the woman. Hiro knew this man was from The World of Souls.

"Anna," the man sighed. "It pains me that we had so little time together in this world."

"I'm sorry, father," Anna said, walking toward him. She reached out to him, but he held up a hand to stop her.

"You can't touch him, Anna," Shampy said from behind her. "It's impossible."

Anna dropped her hands to her side. "I should have gone to you sooner."

"You couldn't," Paudie answered her, "and you know why."

Anna hung her head as if ashamed.

"The answers you've come for …" Paudie said, "I can't give them to you."

Anna shook her head at him. She opened her mouth, possibly to ask for more explanation, but he forestalled her. "What you *need* to know is this: I loved your mother, as I love you. She didn't love me, but we've made amends this past while in The World of Souls. We understand each other much better now and I love both of you all the more for it."

"Father," Anna whispered with tears falling down her cheeks, "what do I do?"

"Remember that I love you. Despite all your questions, I promise that the only thing you need to know is that I love you," Paudie said as he began to fade away. "Love will strengthen and bind us."

When the apparition disappeared, Anna turned tear-stained cheeks to Shampy. "Thank you," she wept.

"Don't thank me, child," the old shaman said, sitting down on the leg of the dead dragon. "My spell didn't work, else your father would have appeared in the fire. He came to you of his own accord."

18

ENEMIES

The pair spent the following night in front of Shampy's little hut. The shaman claimed she would let Anna sleep in her bed inside, but Anna refused. Hiro lay next to her and listened long into the night but he didn't hear the long, slow, deep breathing that usually accompanied her sleep.

Anna sat quietly thoughtful in Hiro's claw the next day as they flew on. Shampy had provided them with food and gave Anna a large shawl that would repel water, but Anna kept it wrapped around her waist in the warm spring air.

Hiro decided it best not to bother her as she reflected on the things her father had shared. He knew grief could be a fickle thing, especially when those feelings are rekindled after a long absence. He would softly ask if she needed to stop and rest or eat or…anything else. For the most part Anna just gazed into the distance or shook her head.

As the pair flew toward the southern border of the Noble Kingdom, Hiro spotted something odd on the horizon. Tilting his tail ever so slightly, he angled toward it.

"Where are we going?" Anna asked, shaken from her reverie.

"I'm still taking you home, but…" Hiro's voice trailed off as they approached the oddly shaped landscape he'd seen. Over a small cluster of hills set between them and the Noble Kingdom, fire smoke in small tendrils reached toward the darkening sky.

Anna peered around Hiro's wrist. "What is it?" she asked.

Hiro didn't answer. He flew on as the sun dipped beyond the horizon.

Finally, when stars began blinking in the dark sky, the misshapen landscape came clear into view.

"Hiro," Anna called up to him, "you have to land, you can't fly over."

"It's dark now," he answered her. "No one will see me."

"They'll have lookouts, Hiro," she insisted. "They *will* see you!"

Before reaching the bright orange speckles on the ground, Hiro settled in a tall tree overlooking the scene. He gently set Anna on a branch above him.

"It's an army," Anna whispered.

"An army?" Hiro asked. He surveyed the sprawl in front of them. He could just make out grayish little domes making the land in front of them seem to bubble. Thousands of them. They stretched as far as he could see into the darkness on either side. The orange lights came from fires burning in carefully selected clearings among the gray domes.

"What are those things?" he asked Anna.

"Tents," she pointed into the sea of them. "Each one can hold up to six men."

Hiro's claw slipped on the trunk. "Six?" If each of those little things held six men, that meant…

"Thousands," Anna voiced his thoughts.

Hiro's maw gaped. What were these men doing? There hadn't been a war involving humans in centuries!

"You know what this means, don't you, Hiro?" Anna asked. Hiro pried his eyes away from the sight in front of them. "These men are marching from the Honorable Kingdom. They're answering Philip's call. They're marching toward the Rock Clouds."

———

"But why would they even bother?" Hiro pointed out again as he pumped his wings. "Humans can't get into the Rock Clouds. Even faeries have a difficult time flying up to Rakgar's lair. The Inner Mountain is the only access they could use and we would surely keep them from climbing too high."

"But," Anna argued, "if any humans do get to the Inner Mountain, they could shoot the dragons on the floating mountains around it. What if they only want to get to the Inner Mountain?"

"For what purpose?"

"Me!" Anna threw her hands in the air. "Have you forgotten that you kidnapped me?"

Hiro shook his head. "But I'm returning you," he said. "Once you're home, Philip will call off any sort of attack, won't he?"

"I don't know," Anna sighed, "he doesn't tell me much. I'm sure he would if he could, but I don't know that the faeries would let him. In any case, I guess we don't have any other choice than to try."

Hiro angled far to the north as they flew. Anna insisted that Philip didn't send many patrols to the mountains anymore, but Hiro gave the Noble Kingdom army a wide course to enter, just to be sure.

"No, wait, it's been weeks," Anna said suddenly from his claw.

Hiro snapped his tail. "It certainly seems like it."

"For that army to gather," Anna continued as if she hadn't heard him, "and be positioned where it is now, Philip would have had to send a request to the Honorable Kingdom weeks ago." Anna's finger swung around in the air as if pointing to positions on a map.

"I took you just over a week ago, almost a fortnight," Hiro said.

"A month," Anna almost whispered.

"It hasn't been a month," Hiro pointed out.

"No, I would say we have a month at best before that army reaches the Rock Clouds," Anna insisted.

"If that's truly where they're going," Hiro added.

To his surprise, Anna nodded. "You're right," she said.

Hiro almost lost his grip on her. He lifted her up to make sure he held the same creature in his claw. "I'm sorry, what did you say?"

She waved away the question. "You're right," she said again, "we need to consider all the options. They're obviously moving north from their home in the south. The request to gather and move had to have come before my abduction. They could, indeed, be headed toward the Noble Kingdom, but for what purpose?

"I don't think they would be waging war on the Noble Kingdom," she continued. She gazed into the dark sky without seeing it. "The Honorable Kingdom is our closest ally. Not to mention, the king is a great friend. He would come immediately when asked, but Philip couldn't possibly have asked him so soon."

"So they're probably not fighting," Hiro conceded, "and they're not here to help rescue you."

"Right," Anna shrugged. "They could just be moving into the Noble Kingdom to assist or join with Noble forces awaiting Philip's orders…or the faeries'."

Hiro thought of something. "Wait, if they wanted to attack dragons, why wouldn't they attack the Desert Ruck? They're much closer to the Honorable Kingdom."

"Just south of it, actually; straight over the desert," Anna said.

"So why journey north to kill dragons?"

"Because that seems to be where Philip is waging his war," Anna answered. "Besides, it would be the best place to start. Attack the dragons in the center of Avonoa; those not killed would flee to the other rucks most likely. Then each kingdom could attack the ruck closest to them."

Hiro thought back to the meeting with the centaurs. "The arrows, Anna," he groaned and she shifted in his claw to look up at him. "If your brother equips that army with those arrows…"

Anna's arm around Hiro's wrist clamped down tighter, "The dragons won't stand a chance."

After the moons had risen and followed their path across a good portion of the night sky, Anna called up to Hiro.

"I think we should set down for the night," she said. She kept her voice low.

Hiro nodded. He circled with one wing tilted toward the ground. He couldn't make out much in the darkness, but he wouldn't tell Anna. They were north of the route he had followed when he had come to "kidnap" the princess several days past. Directly beneath them, jagged boulders churned as if rolling around a boiling pot. Hiro angled away from the boulders to land in a thick patch of Klynn trees. As soon as his claws touched the ground, he froze.

"This is wrong," he whispered. He stared into the trees, but did more listening than searching with his eyes. "We shouldn't be here." He heard no animal noises, big or small. But he caught a whiff of a scent he couldn't place. Something familiar…but wrong.

Anna had been ready to slide out of his front claw when they touched down. She was accustomed to standing still until Hiro declared it was safe, but she teetered on the edge of his talons when he spoke.

"What do you mean?" she asked. "Is it not safe?" She twisted her neck to peer into the trees around them as well. "Is something out—?"

She also froze and didn't continue. Hiro had closed his eyes and was trying to place the scent in the air. When he realized she hadn't finished her sentence, he opened his eyes. Looking down at the little human, he saw her wide eyes staring behind them. He turned to follow her gaze.

Behind them, in what he had assumed were boulders on the edge of the cluster of trees, were unmistakable ruins. Walls with gaping windows like vacant eyes stared back at them. Doorways like screaming mouths warned them away.

"Someone lived here," he whispered into the dark, but Anna jumped down from his claw and stepped up to the ruins.

"Not just anyone," she whispered back. She lowered herself on her heels next to an opening in the rocks. Even when she squatted, the opening that started at the ground barely came up to her nose.

"Goblins," Hiro hissed. Anna's shaking hand crept closer to the rock walls. Hiro searched the ruined walls for signs of life or movement. "Anna," he whispered, "we should leave. Now."

But she didn't move. "Hiro," she whispered back, "they could help us."

He narrowed his eyes at her. "Have you lost your mind?" he hissed again. "Don't you remember the last time we met goblins?"

"King Svorgh," she said, her eyes glazed, obviously remembering the cryptic messages and actions of the goblin king. "He's powerful." She finally pulled her hovering fingers away from the rocks and turned to look back at the dragon. "Even Shvika could overpower you. If they can do that, they could help us fight the humans and faeries."

"And who's to say they will?" he growled, stepping closer to her. "The last time we met them, Svorgh made us swear on each other's lives that we wouldn't tell anyone about them."

"But the stones they wear," Anna insisted, "they wield the power of another army by themselves."

"But what will they ask in return?" Hiro turned his eyes toward the ruins, but they were focused on a green dragon far away. "If we show up asking favors, they might just kill us, assuming we had told others about them."

"They might not," Anna shook her head. "They let us go last time."

Hiro's eyes drifted to Anna. He remembered her bound with a sword pressed to her throat by the little blue-skinned goblin with thick arms. His heart tightened at the thought. "Nothing in their behavior makes me believe they would do the same thing twice, and I have no desire to *attempt*—" he emphasized the word, "—to renew that vow." He turned away from the ruins and tip-taloned partway back to the trees. If the goblins were anywhere nearby, he didn't want them to know that he was here too. "I'm leaving," he said over his shoulder. "Are you coming with me?"

Anna stood up, not taking her eyes off the stones in front of her, and stepped backward toward Hiro. As his eyes grew accustomed to the low light, they could both see that this collection of boulders had at one time been a small goblin village. Hiro's tongue felt dry at the musky scent of the goblins. Lichen crawled from between the stones. Many of the stones from the walls had tumbled down or been swallowed in the soft ground. He could only guess what majikal horrors lay within.

Once Anna was close enough, Hiro scooped her up and threw her onto his back. Normally he would've jumped from the ruins into the sky, but he didn't dare get closer to anything goblin-made. He turned away from the goblin village and bounded away into the trees.

19

NONCONFORMING

"Snorks?" Hiro snorted a laugh as they soared through the sky. "Why would anyone eat snorks?" After exhausting the subjects of the army, arrows, dragons, and faeries as they flew, Hiro had resorted to overwhelming Anna with questions about humans to keep her from worrying over past events. Riddles had begun duplicating and Anna knew almost too much about dragons already. So with Hiro feigning interest in human life, they continued their playful pettifog as he glid on the warm spring air.

"They're a delicacy in the Just Kingdom," Anna answered with a huff, "although I've been taught never to accept any from a Clan Mother. I've tasted them and they're not that bad. A little on the sweet side, but quite tasty. It just depends on how you cook them."

"That's the problem, though, isn't it?" Hiro pointed out. "If a dragon were to 'cook them,' they would end up a small burnt dot. Not worth eating any more than the logs they live under."

"Yet you'll eat the heart of a lion."

"Lion hearts are very good."

"They're poisonous to humans."

Hiro chuckled again. "Snorks aren't poisonous to dragons, but I still wouldn't bother eating them." He flew silently for a bit and then asked, "Why can't you accept snorks from a Clan Mother?"

"I don't remember for certain," she hemmed, "but I think it has something to do with passing out and waking up glowing iridescent like the snork trails."

Hiro roared with laughter. When he could speak again, he sputtered, "One of these days we must go to the Just Kingdom and learn the truth from those Clan Mothers."

"I hear they're very secretive and extremely fierce. That's how they obtain their status, practically by force," she told him.

Hiro nodded. "Sounds much like a dragon."

Anna hemmed, "It does, doesn't it? Except I'm sure the Clan Mothers aren't nearly as bull-headed."

"Bull-headed," Hiro repeated slowly, feeling the word in his mouth. "What is that supposed to mean?"

"Bull-headed?" Anna shook her head. "It means you, you big, stubborn bull."

Hiro looked down at the woman in his fist with a crease in his brow.

"A claxio bull," she clarified, "if confronted by a wall, would knock its head against the wall trying to force it out of the way. Even if the wall were no more than a few paces wide and easily surpassed, the bull would die trying to force the thing from its path before ever taking a few steps to the side to go around it. Stupidity until death. Claxios are not very bright at all."

Hiro glared down at the woman. "Claxios are also small, furry creatures that can't fly. A dragon is much larger and stronger. Although we could fly over it, we would more wisely knock the wall down and walk over it."

She crossed her arms. "Like I said, bull-headed."

Hiro opened his mouth to explain how being able to knock the wall down had nothing to do with being stubborn, but Anna sat up straight in his fist. "Hiro," she said quietly, "I see smoke in the mountains." She pointed toward where they had taken the route through the mountains when they left.

Hiro shook his head. "We need to land anyway," he whispered.

Anna clung to his front leg as they spiraled downward. Hiro must have been distracted by their conversation because they were much further into the Torthoth Mountains than he had planned to be by now. Once they'd landed he swung Anna up to his back, where she wrapped her arms around his neck. Hiro tucked her legs under his wings to keep her in place and took off running up the mountain at a gallop.

Anna sat away from his back rather than be bounced against it as he ran. He scanned the mountainside for danger, watching around them more than where he put his claws. He assumed the woman was keeping an eye out as well, but dragons could see much greater detail and much further than humans could. He raced for the top of the mountain before the sun could disappear behind it completely.

He bounced from boulder to boulder, his course taking them further north to avoid the wisps of smoke Anna had pointed out. The pair travelled in silence until they circled around the north side of the peak and could see the valley beyond the range.

Hiro stood still. The sun hovered as if within reach partway through its descent. It burned bright and at just the right angle for his sharp day vision to see something out of the ordinary.

"What is it?" Anna whispered. "What do you see?"

"I'm not sure," Hiro hemmed, "it looks like a road or passage of some sort."

The way the mountain to the south of them bulged, they still couldn't see the source of the smoke. Anna pointed this out. "We won't be seen if you stay low," she told him. "If it's a road, I can find my way home from there."

They were much further north of her home than Hiro dared leave her, but if someone were burning a fire nearby, they would be able to help her. He nodded and allowed an upper current to lift him to just above the treetops.

Close to the trees, the air current wasn't steady enough to glide. Hiro's tail whipped around, trying to keep him on a somewhat mild course. Anna's arms strangled him as she tried to stay attached. He kept her on his back until they landed at the base of the mountain range, inside the Noble Kingdom.

"This isn't a road," Anna's voice dropped, "but someone has definitely been through here."

Hiro crept closer to what he could now clearly see were the tracks of thousands of boot prints and wagon ruts in the mud. "Many someones," he reasoned. From his earlier perch on the mountain he could see the separation in the trees but he couldn't make out the muddy ground.

Pressing his nose almost into the mud, he tried to pull apart the many scents assaulting him. "Humans," he said.

Anna nodded, kneeling on a clump of dry grass alongside the prints. "Hundreds of them."

"Another army?" Hiro questioned.

"Not quite that many," Anna answered, "but still quite a few men."

Hiro pointed to the wagon marks. "One group came through with wagons a long time ago. Weeks, maybe months." He pointed to the prints around the wagons, then the ones trampling over them. "More came through just days ago. I can still smell their breath." Noting the position of the toes of their boots, he lifted his nose to face north. "I could catch up to them."

Anna stood up and he turned to face her. "I won't make you take me with you, Hiro." She clamped her hands at her waist. "But I would like to go. I know Philip and the faeries are planning something and I want to help you."

"I have no idea how dangerous this could be," he warned her. Yet, in his mind, he hated to leave her on a lesser-used road where it was possible that no one might venture for several days or weeks.

"It would be more dangerous for you, as a dragon." She took a step toward him, ignoring the squelching mud around her soft boots. "If they see me with you, you can drop me and they'll think they rescued me. But they might still try to kill you."

"Alright," he nodded, "I don't want to leave you here, not knowing if any help will come by."

Without a word, the woman ran through the mud to jump toward his back. He caught her in mid-air and lifted her the rest of the way. The pair ran through the trees in the setting sun, with Hiro keeping his nose to the ground.

20

BEDEVILED PURSUIT

"Mother!" Tierni's voice echoed off the walls, slicing the silence that met her in their family's home entry. "Mother!" she bellowed, planting her fists on her hips.

"Is everything alright, Miss Tierni?"

Tierni spun at the sound of the voice. George. He had been with them since Tierni was a child, one of the few servants they retained. A patient, kind man and one of the only people who could deal with Tierni when she was enraged. She saw Martha disappear around the corner behind him; she cowered from anyone who sounded angry. But somehow, their presence calmed Tierni…slightly.

"I need to speak to my mother," she seethed, pulling her cloak from her shoulders. "Do you know where she is?"

"I'm not positive," George answered, keeping his voice low and soft, "but she might still be upstairs. Your brother was just here—"

Tierni didn't want to hear what her rotten troll of a brother had been doing here. This was the first chance Tierni had had to get away from work in the castle. She had fumed. She had raged to her friends in the laundry. She had received some good advice from Mistress Kay. Now that she had a respite, she had come to speak to her mother. She bounded up the stairs two at a time, ignoring George's gasp when she hiked her skirts above her knees.

They didn't have a large house, but it was comfortable and situated close enough to the palace for convenience. Most of her father's, Royal General Bragon's, fortune had been used to further Torgon's career. Money poorly spent it seemed, considering how many times he had been tested and passed but denied a promotion purportedly because of his young age. She'd since heard her parents discuss Riddig's and Murzod's vendetta against their family and it made her blood boil.

Riddig was Murzod's uncle, and those two still thought Riddig should have been the Royal General rather than Bragon. Now that Torgon had surpassed Murzod in ranking and caused him to lose status, the intensity of the feud had doubled. For years Riddig foul-mouthed Bragon behind his back. Now Murzod continued the tradition with Torgon. If either Riddig or Murzod had their way, Tierni's family line would be extinct.

Tierni burst into the small sitting room on the second floor. "There you are!" Her mother's small frame was silhouetted against the soft blue curtains, but Tierni didn't give her a chance to speak before launching into a tirade. "George said that Torgon came to see you. That's fine. Now you'll hear my side of it whether you want to hear it or not."

She drew herself up to her full height. "It's bad enough that I've been stuck in the castle laundry, but when I finally get a chance to meet someone new …" She spotted a vase on the table next to her and her fingers idly circled the rim. "I mean, I don't know whether anything would happen between the two of us. Yes, I've always admired him from a distance, since I'm not allowed anywhere near him." She thrust her hands behind her back to keep herself from launching the vase across the room.

Turning on her heel, she paced the few steps across the room in front of her mother. "He's a very nice young man. Father has always said so himself. I mean, really, he's Torgon's best friend!" She pointed to a family portrait hanging over the fireplace. "What could he possibly have against me eating dinner with the king?"

"Tierni," her mother whispered.

"I know," Tierni waved her hand at her mother as she turned slowly to face her. "I know, I haven't been trained as a noble, but it's not like I'm lying about my status." She absent-mindedly picked up a couple of books sitting on a shelf. "The king himself insisted on inviting me to dinner! How could Torgon force me to leave like that?!" She dropped the books with more force than she meant.

"He wouldn't even let me embarrass myself! It's not like my mistakes would reflect directly on him." Having made her way back across the room, she dusted at imagined bits on the fireplace mantle. "Indirectly, maybe, but everyone at the table would know I hadn't been trained!" Finally dropping all pretenses, she folded her arms across her chest.

"It's not fair and you know it! I'm just as smart as Torgon! I'm every bit as noble as any other noble in the kingdom, with or without training! I suspect even the king sees that!" She ground her teeth and inspected the floor. "How can you let him do this to me, Mother?" She realized how long she had been rambling. "Mother? Are you even listening to me?"

When Tierni met her mother's eyes she saw streaks of tears down her cheeks. Her eyes were red and swollen. She held a piece of paper in one hand and a handcloth reduced to a wad in the other. "Your brother, Torgon, has gone."

"I know he's gone," Tierni stood still, uncomprehending, "probably back to his plush little office in the palace."

Her mother shook her head and sat gently in the chair beside her. She lifted the paper toward Tierni while blotting at her eyes with the spent handcloth. "It's his directive."

His directive. Saying who should get all the money from the estate should the worst happen. Tierni had seen them before, from her father.

"But that doesn't mean anything," Tierni said. "Father had to fill in a new one every time he left for an assignment, no matter how mundane." She folded her arms again and jutted her chin toward the window. "Probably leaving to visit an exotic country with the king.

He'll be sipping wine in the Just Kingdom, watching dancing girls while you worry about him."

"He's going to..." her voice cracked, "... to The Great Northern Mountain, Tierni," her mother whispered the name, and for good reason.

Tierni's face snapped to her mother's. "Isn't that...?" Her mother nodded. Tierni's jaw dropped in realization. After a moment of consideration, all anger toward her brother drained as if she'd walked muddy through a waterfall. She ran to her mother. Falling to her knees on the floor, she threw her arms around her mother's waist and buried her own sobbing face in her skirts.

He had gone. Torgon had gone to the one place from which older soldiers believed no one would ever return. Not only had he gone to the Cursed Mountain, but also straight into the arms of his own feuding enemy. Anything could happen when Torgon faced Murzod. And Tierni was certain Murzod would see to it that something did.

—

"We'll rest here tonight," Hiro said, stopping next to a clump of trees.

The path they followed stayed close to the base of the mountain. Anna had surmised in the light that the tracks they followed had to be from Noble soldiers. Most of the lines were uniform and the boots were made of the same cut and shape. They even found a discarded arrow shaft with blue fletching similar to those used by Noble soldiers.

"We haven't come very far," Anna said once she slid from his back. "Are you sure we shouldn't keep going through the night?"

Hiro shook his head and curled up next to a clump of hytocomp. "We'll have to conserve our energy," he told her. "The temperatures drop very low at night in the spring. I can feel the air is much cooler this far north as well. I'll have to be careful how much fire I use in the cold air."

Anna ripped out a handful of hytocomp to fill her water skin. The plant bulged from soaking up the melting snows and quickly filled her bag. Sitting down next to the black dragon, she mumbled with a grin, "Don't tell me dragons *aren't* invincible!"

"More so than humans," he nudged her with his shoulder, spilling her water. He chuckled when she cursed and stood to retrieve more hytocomp. But his brow creased as she sat down again. "Will you be warm enough with just that cloak around you?"

She shook some excess water from her hands, splashing him in the face. "I will be as long as I'm not wet," she hissed.

Hiro gazed into the distance. "The further north we travel, the more snow and ice we'll find," he said, "and the closer we'll get to the Ice Ruck."

Anna fumbled the last of the hytocomp but tried to cover herself. "Ice Ruck," she spluttered, "you mean ice dragons exist too?"

He frowned at her. "Of course they exist."

She frowned too. "But if ice dragons live in the cold, why is it so dangerous to you? Shouldn't you be able to live in the cold too?"

Hiro rolled his shoulder. "Ice dragons are much better acclimated to the cold. A dragon from any other ruck must travel extremely slowly to the north and gradually adjust to the temperatures. Or travel in the winter. But once ice dragons are used to the cold temperatures, they don't like to leave the cold weather. I've heard that their scales and bodies adapt so completely to the cold that they can then warm too much or too quickly if they travel to the south, and that can be dangerous for them. They don't leave their ruck often and they don't get many visitors."

Anna settled back against his warm body. "How do their bodies adapt?"

"I've only heard stories," he shrugged. "Some say their scales grow as thick as armor. Some say they get thinner and multiply a thousand times over. The thinner scales become so numerous that they look like feathers."

"Feathers?"

"They're just stories," Hiro laid his head on his claw. "I'm sure they still look like dragons. Besides, we have no reason to go discover the truth for ourselves."

The next night they slept in snow. Tufts of grass and plants were exposed as the snow melted through the night from Hiro's warmth and the warmth of a fire, but Hiro woke several times shivering in the dark. He woke to memories of being chained in a courtyard. He woke to memories of ice-cold pain shooting through his claws and up his arms. When he woke, he shook from the cold and couldn't go back to sleep.

"Why aren't you sleeping?" Anna whispered in the dark.

"I thought I heard something," Hiro lied. "How did you know I wasn't asleep?"

"The snoring stopped," Anna said, snuggling deeper into her cloak.

Hiro pulled another small tree into the fire, shaking his head. "I don't snore."

Anna turned narrowed eyes on him. "Are you joking?" She propped herself up on one elbow. "Everyone knows dragons snore. And you must be the worst one yet."

"Dragons most certainly do not snore." He laid his head on his claws to attempt to go back to sleep.

"Oh, I see," Anna nodded, curling back into her cloak, "the noise must be all those walls you knock down in your sleep, then."

—

The next day the sun burned over their head but gave them little relief from the cold. Hiro growled with frustration. "We don't seem any closer to catching up to the humans." He bent his head over the tracks to smell the men. Their scent was still fresh, but he thought they must be moving much faster than he realized. "I have a much longer stride and no need to stop as often as they might. How are they remaining so far ahead of us?"

"Majik?" Anna suggested. "They are working with faeries. Perhaps the faeries are helping them speed on."

"Perhaps," Hiro said, "but every step we take makes our journey more dangerous. I don't know how much longer we can last."

Anna slid her hand down his neck. "You need to eat. Maybe you'll move faster if you have more fire."

"There's nothing to eat up here," he rumbled at her. He licked his frozen claws to try to get feeling back into them. "I haven't smelled any passing animals all day, nor did I yesterday. I won't have anything to hunt."

"Then we must go back," Anna said. "You can't go on like this. I feel you shiver at night. I know your senses aren't working as well as they normally would."

"No!" Hiro yelled. "This is the best lead we've had to discover what is going on. We can't just abandon it."

When he started moving again, Anna leaned over his neck. "Three days," she whispered. "We can give it three more days, but if we don't find anything more, we turn around. Agreed?"

"And if I say 'No'?" he growled at her.

She sat up straight, swaying on his back. Hiro could practically hear her hands on her hips. "Then I'll walk back by myself and get help to collect your stubborn ashes."

21

YIELDING TO A FISSURE

After another day-and-a-half of running through the sparsely growing trees, Hiro came to a sudden halt. Anna sat up on his back and the two of them stared in silence. In front of them, the boot prints they'd been following diverged in two directions.

Hiro, sniffing, first followed the prints turning to the left. They turned west into the trees and the mountains beyond. Then he wriggled backward to the point of divergence and followed the other prints to the north a few paces. He could feel the air getting colder as he watched the tracks disappear ahead of him into the frozen northern wasteland. His eyes widened as he sniffed the tracks leading north.

"Now what?" Anna asked as the dragon slithered back to where the two tracks started. "Which ones do we follow?"

"I'm not sure," Hiro answered honestly. "The ones moving west are still fresh. The ones moving north are less so, but there's one major difference."

"The tracks," Anna shifted from side to side comparing the boot prints.

"The tracks going west have prints leading both away from us and back toward us," Hiro pointed out. "The tracks going north..."

"...only lead north," Anna whispered. "No one returns from the north."

"If we follow them, we might not come back," Hiro rumbled.

"If we go west," Anna said, sitting up straighter, "we risk coming to a dead end, having to double back, or heading deeper into the Courageous Kingdom without finding them. If we follow the ones to the north—"

"—we risk death from cold," Hiro finished flatly. His leg joints shook from the thought of worse cold to come.

"I think we should go west," Anna shifted on his back to peer toward where the tracks led. "I'll be fine. You have more chance of finding food along the way."

"No," Hiro said, loping down the tracks heading north, "there's another difference in the tracks."

"What's that?"

"The ones leading north have a fresh scent of lion crossing them."

Hiro suddenly darted through stunted bushes and dwarfed trees, off the trail of the human prints. Anna clung to his back as he sprinted northeast. He slowed when he saw pines as tall as two dragons and as wide as three. He shrugged Anna from his back.

"Stay here," he told her, setting her on her feet by a few short trees. "They might try to hurt you if you're with me, but they'll run past if they're fleeing an attack. Just try not to draw their attention. I'll be back."

Lions loved two things, cold and pine. Hiro could smell them beyond the pines. He could hear their hearts pounding a strong rhythm, each in harmony with the others. He didn't need to eat many. Albik lions were large. Their six strong legs had enough meat to feed Hiro's fire for several weeks. Although they were half his size, he could easily kill all of them if need be. Possibly the entire pack of eight.

He burst through the trees with a roar. The lions froze momentarily and he was able to catch one before the others hissed and scattered. When he finished his kill, he returned to Anna with blood dripping down his chin.

Anna stood by the trees where he'd left her. She hadn't moved. She stared wide-eyed into the sky beyond the pines.

Hiro approached her cautiously. He could tell that the lions hadn't come near because he saw no lion prints in the snow around her. So why did she continue staring past Hiro with terror in her eyes?

"Are you alright?" Hiro asked.

The woman nodded. "We won't have to get any closer, will we?" she whispered.

Hiro's brow creased. He snaked his head around to search for what mesmerized her. Beyond the pines he could see something familiar against the crystal blue sky.

Several wingfalls away, but less than a day as the dragon flies, a mountain range rose to scratch the sky. He walked away from Anna to get a better view.

On the other side of the pines, a white expanse stretched before them until it met the base of the mountains. From here, with his sharp eyes, he could see movement in the mountains. The mountains themselves were covered mostly in white but Hiro could see dragons flying over and through the tips of the mountains. He could see several of them. The Northern Ice Ruck.

"No," he shook his head, joining Anna again. He used his claw to help her onto his back and spun around. He ran toward the track of human prints in the snow. "There's no reason to get any closer."

With his belly full and his fire burning bright, Hiro galloped along the track. The stench of human men grew stronger with every step. As did the cold. Hiro's nose felt like solid ice. His tongue hung on the side of his face as he breathed hot air to warm himself.

"Hiro, please slow down," Anna begged.

"How can you ask that," he repeated, "when you know we're finally catching up?"

"We can't just run into them," she said, "we have to take them by surprise. We have to find out what they're up to first, then decide what to do."

Hiro lessened his run to a steady trot. "What do you mean?"

"If we run into the men…" Anna's words slurred from her frozen lips, "… don't you think it would be best for me to go in and find out what they're doing? You can't just take them all on!"

Hiro stopped. "I'm not sending you in to do anything," he growled.

"I'm not asking your permission," Anna growled back. "What are you going to do? Slip quietly into their camp or stop someone passing by to ask a few questions?"

Hiro sighed, then rolled his shoulder. "What would you suggest we do?"

"The sun is going down," she pointed out, "you caught up to them much faster with more fire in you. I think we should rest the night and discuss our next move."

At least she wasn't telling him what to do, or what she was going to do. He loped away from the track toward some shorter pines. He ripped some smaller trees from the ground and dragged them into the middle of the pines.

"These should give adequate cover," he said, indicating the pines just over his head. He put Anna on the ground and set the tree ablaze. With the fire going, he realized just how dark the sky was getting.

Anna pulled her legs to her chest with her bag in front of her. After rummaging through it, she produced a small, yellowish-brown lump. "What I wouldn't give for some soup to go with this," she mumbled before tearing at it with her teeth.

"Soup?" Hiro asked, curling on the ground next to her.

"Mmmm," she nodded, "fick brof, wif cawwos as bik as me fisk." She held up her closed fist for emphasis, although Hiro had to decipher the rest of the statement around her mouthful of food.

"Carrots?"

"Hmmmm," she closed her eyes, thinking about the hot soup. After she swallowed, she continued. "Carrots. A purple root plant grown in fields like Jarek's."

Hiro shivered, but not from the cold. "Eww, plants again. Don't you ever eat meat?"

Anna scrunched her face and jerked a thick strip of meat from her bag, then shoved it back in. "Humans can't subsist on meat alone. It would kill us."

"Weakling," he taunted, but indicated the lump in her hand. "Then what are you eating?"

"Bread," she said as she took another chunk from it.

"What's bread?"

"Mosslee wet," she said while chewing.

"Wet moss?"

She shook her head with a grin and swallowed. "Mostly wheat. Although moss is quite tasty when prepared properly. Wheat is a grain, grown—"

"Let me guess," he interrupted, "in a field like Jarek's."

She shrugged, nodded, and ripped into the bread again.

"Sounds to me like humans couldn't live long without people like Jarek," he said, laying his head on his claws.

"Very true." She waited before she put another chunk of bread in her mouth. "I've been trying to convince people like my brother of that for some time."

"Perhaps if you weren't so mean all the time, people would listen to you."

"I'm nice to you and you still don't listen to me."

Hiro leveled his eyes to hers, "I'm not 'people,' I'm a dragon."

"You're right," she nodded, "you're much more stubborn."

Hiro grinned. "Do you have any ideas about what we should do when we find these humans we're looking for?"

"Actually, I do," she nodded and placed the remnants of the bread back into her bag. "I was thinking that I could wander into their camp…"

Hiro listened as she spelled out a plan to pretend that she had been lost or kidnapped and ask the men for help. They would willingly take her in, most likely, and making her status known, she would gain access to the highest ranking men and pump them for answers as to their mission.

It's a good plan, Hiro confessed to himself. *She's not a threat by herself. Her royalty should allow her to learn all we need to know. She's smart. As smart as Priya.*

He grinned at that. Priya would hate him for comparing the two of them. He could hear the dame's voice in his head.

How could you possibly compare a dragon and a human? He could even hear the dangerous growl in her voice. He could see her posturing to pounce on him. She wouldn't stand for such a demeaning idea.

"What are you grinning at?" Anna's voice cut through his thoughts.

"I was just thinking about how similar you are to Priya," he answered honestly.

Anna pursed her lips. "I could never be that cruel."

Hiro rolled his shoulder. "Priya's not cruel. Strict? Absolutely. But never cruel."

Anna shook her head and turned to stare into the burning tree branches. "You probably find her brand of cruelty entertaining."

"She's good for a laugh," he nudged her with his tail, "just like you."

Anna rolled her eyes at the fire. Hiro rested his head on his claws. Anna was smart. Priya was smart. Why couldn't the two get along? Anna was nicer than many dragons. Maybe Priya thought she was too nice? No, it always came down to the rules with Priya. She followed rules to everyone's detriment. Hiro had never been able to tempt her. But Anna almost enjoyed breaking rules.

A thought struck Hiro as he stared into the fire beside Anna. *What if Priya and Anna switched minds?* He chuckled to himself.

Anna was beautiful, for a human. She had soft skin and swirling yellow hair—even when it was pasted to her head from rain or frozen in clumps from the cold. But her bright green eyes were the best part of her. Those eyes! They were the exact color of Priya's scales.

But as beautiful as Anna was, it was really her rebellious, curious, kind, persistent attitude that made her quite endearing. Priya's mind in Anna's body would be brilliant, no doubt, but Anna's personality in Priya's body...?

CRACK!

22

TROTH

"OH SPIT!" Hiro yelled, bounding to his feet.

"I beg your pardon!" Her eyes pierced his.

Those eyes! Those beautiful eyes! He shook his head to empty the thoughts. He hadn't even realized his heart was hardening! *But her soft hair…skin. No!* "Oh, spit in Tarsa's eye!" he said, stumbling backward away from her.

"What's gotten into you?" She hugged her shoulders when he moved away, sapping his warmth from her limbs.

Hiro reached toward her to curl her into his arms and warm her, but froze. His eyes twitched. His claws curled and uncurled. He stared wild-eyed when he felt a hard lump wriggle up from somewhere into the deep bottom of his throat.

"Oh spit! Oh SPIT! OH SPIT!" he murmured, squirming his tail into the trees behind him, but reaching for her at the same time. His very limbs fought against each other!

"What's wrong with you?!" Anna stood up to follow him. "What's going on?"

Her brow creased in concern. He marveled at how the cold reddening her cheeks made her seem cheerful. Oh, Tartaku, how he wanted to stay with her, but the lump rose further into his throat.

"Nothing's wrong," he coughed, and the lump wedged along his neck. He spun to search for which way to go.

Get away! I have to get away from her! He tumbled horn-over-tail into the trees surrounding their little camp, desperately pushing away thoughts of the warmth and comfort beside her.

"Where are you going?" she called at him through the branches.

"Stay here," he coughed as the lump reached further up his throat. "I'll be right back!" he choked before dashing away into the trees.

He didn't know how long he ran. The hard lump slipped into his mouth, but he kept running with his jaws clamped tight. With only a vague idea, he knew he couldn't run north; the humans were that way. He couldn't run east; the Ice Ruck was there. South would be backtracking and a waste of time; so he ran west. Into the mountains, higher and higher. He stopped when he realized the mountain beneath him was sloping around the far west side and down again. He collapsed in the snow.

Wake up, he barked to himself. *Wake up! Open your eyes! It's not true. It's all a dream. A nightmare! It's impossible!*

He rolled the lump on his tongue. He thought of the pull in his heart toward Anna. Despite her many failings. Despite her sharp words—all meant in jest. Despite her frail human body—more attractive every second. Despite her disgusting human habits—those didn't seem so bad anymore either. This couldn't happen. It had to be impossible! But denying it didn't help. Hiro finally rolled his shoulder and opened his mouth.

The teardrop-shaped, faceted black gem fell out and dropped into the snow at his feet, making the moisture hiss into his face. Both Priya's and Anna's eyes seemed to mock him from its dark depths.

How is this possible? He stared at the smooth-cut surface of his heart. *How could my heart break for a human? After all this time protecting it? After it not breaking for Priya? Oh, what will Priya say? Can I even tell her?*

He stood staring at his own heart. The sun passed overhead. How many times? He couldn't be sure. All he knew was that at one point the sun glinted from one of the facets into his eye and he wished it could be strong enough to burn him to ash right there.

What happens now? he thought, staring into the sun reflected in the heart in front of him. *Anna's skin is as warm as the sun sometimes. Will I ever be able to enjoy it? Will I ever hold her and not worry about her dying because I hold her? Speak to her? Love her?*

I do love her, don't I? he growled at himself. Should he be mad at himself? Happy? He should be happy because his heart had finally broken. He no longer needed to protect it. *It's now hers to protect. Will she?* he wondered to himself.

Shampy! Hiro perked up thinking of the creature. *A spell maybe. Could she restore my heart?* He froze. *Do I want her to?* He thought back to several dragons he knew whose hearts had broken for undeserving heart collectors. The stories passed among dans as warnings. Those dans had tried everything to sever the ties to those dames, but in vain.

"No spell, no prayers, no amount of anger or hatred can restore your heart," his father Tusten had taught him. "This is why you must make certain your heart breaks for a dame who deserves your loyalty."

Am I a traitor? A blood and ash traitor? He sighed. *Do I even deserve to turn to ash when I die? I can't tell anyone. Will anyone ever find out? Should I even tell Anna?*

Stars sparkled on the facets of the heart. His eyes wanted to close, but he couldn't keep them from opening again to stare at the heart. He loved how Anna's eyes sparkled in the dark. The green of her eyes was so bright that sometimes he could see it in the dark.

Ashel told me I would be influenced by the Star of Love. Had she known? Was she warning me? He flopped onto the ground. *Tog knew. He didn't trust me with her. But did he ever believe this would happen?* His shoulder began to ache from rolling it so much.

I'll never have hatchlings. Hiro's eyes threatened to leak. *Anna and I will never be able to make this heart into an egg together.* It was the greatest goal of a dan to be a father, and a good one. With Anna, Hiro would never experience that joy.

Could Anna and I even live together? Will I ever see her again? She must live in Kingstor, and her brother tries to kill me every time I come near the Noble Kingdom.

Lying on the frozen mountain floor in the dark, Hiro felt his stomach lurch. He grew cold. How long had he been here? Was Anna okay where he had left her? He bounced to his feet at the thought of the woman then pursed his lips at his behavior. He truly was in love with that beast.

Of all the creatures to love ... bile rose into his throat. *I used to hate humans. Not many months ago, I trained hatchlings to hate humans. I would have been better off falling in love with a unicorn! At least unicorns have beautiful manes.* He thought of Anna's hair, now matted with dirt and unkempt, but he still longed to brush it against his cheek.

The other half of his heart, still in his body, pulled him toward her. He knew her exact direction. *I have a feeling that even if she moved, I still might know where she was. But why? How can I love her so? She's just a human!*

She's kind, he answered his own question without meaning to. *She's compassionate. She can be jovial, but thoughtful. She was and is willing to help me and listen to me when no one else will. She's put herself in danger for me repeatedly. But she's also strong, willful, and won't let anyone tell her what to do.*

Perhaps, it finally dawned on him with a new sun overhead, *perhaps I can love her without our being together. She will have to live her life. I will have to allow it. I will have to slowly and painfully figure out how to continue mine. Without her.*

She's not completely unworthy, he thought. *She won't abuse my heart. I know that. She won't tell others, because she'll know the severity of the consequences. I know that too. He could do nothing else but give it to her.*

He shook his head and scooped up the heart from the forest floor. He turned toward the camp, but his stomach cramped. The fire in his belly guttered and threatened to disappear altogether. He didn't know what else to do, so he belched a flame to make sure his fire was indeed still there. It melted the snow in front of him and lit a few twigs on fire. When he stopped, the fire in his belly—next to where the other half of his heart still remained—burned as strong as ever.

Perhaps this always happens after your heart breaks, he thought of his guttering fire as he started back toward Anna. *But it's gone now.*

He flew back to Anna, skirting the treetops with his tail. Carrying the lump of glossy black gemstone in his claw felt like he dragged the entire mountain along with him. He saw no one along the way. No humans. No dragons. It was as if the rest of the world had disappeared, and that was just as well.

The sun glowed overhead when he landed, but it still gave no warm relief. Had he been gone the whole night? He pushed through the trees.

At first he didn't see her. A pile of ashes lay within the trees with a lump of snow next to them, which he assumed was the remainder of the log to burn. But he noticed Anna's foot jutting out from underneath.

He raced to her side, growling at himself. "Anna," he whispered. He set down the heart and lifted her with one claw. The other claw reached for one of the nearby trees. Nothing else within reach would burn. He tore off branches and lit them on fire as he inspected her face. Although she had thrown Shampy's water-repellant cloth over her head, her cheeks had drained of color and grown pale. Her lips had gone from pink to the same pale blue as the unforgiving sky. "Anna?" he whispered, curling both claws around her and setting her down close to the burning branches.

Her iced lashes fluttered open. She groaned, but Hiro couldn't decipher what she said.

"Stay here," he said, settling her next to the fire, "I'll get more to burn." Lifting into the air, he twisted in all directions. Further north he saw a large, fallen tree. He couldn't drag the entire mass to her side, but he burned off enough of it to bring back and warm them for a while.

Hiro didn't rest easy until Anna began to stir under his claw as they lay next to the fire. "Hiro?" she croaked.

"I'm here," he murmured. "Are you alright?"

"Where did you go?" She raised a hand to her head. "You were gone so long."

"I'm sorry," he hung his head. "I'm so sorry."

"Where did you go?" her voice dropped to a dangerously low pitch.

He rolled his shoulder. "There was something I had to do."

Anna grunted as she pushed herself up to sitting. Those brilliant green eyes bore into his. "And?"

"And what?"

She wrapped her cloak tighter around her shoulders, but her eyes never left his. Finally she turned her head to the burning fire. "You were gone for days." Her voice was low but steady.

"I'm sorry."

"Sorry?" She squirmed out of his grip to stand in front of the fire. "Sorry?" She pinched her arms together around herself and spun on the dragon. Those beautiful eyes looked like they were on fire. "You disappear for days with no explanation and all you have to say for yourself is you're sorry?!"

"I left you with a fire," he defended himself, gesturing to the burning log.

"I couldn't gather firewood on my own! The fire burned out after only a day!" she yelled. "Perhaps I should've gone after the humans on my own!"

"Perhaps," he whispered.

"And now you come back and all you have to say is that you're sorry?!" she repeated with incredulity. Her gruff whisper hurt more than a scream.

He scratched at the ground, the black lump of his heart felt like it was stabbing into his back behind him. "I told you, I had something to do."

"What, Hiro?" She opened her hands in front of her to implore of him, but quickly pressed them back against her body. "What was so important that you left me here on my own to die?"

"This!" he bellowed back. Before he could stop himself, Hiro bounded to his feet and hurled the lump of black stone at Anna's stomach. She doubled over with a loud huff of air, but caught it in both hands.

She straightened to glare at Hiro through narrowed eyes. "How dare you?!" she hissed. "How dare you gather treasure while I'm trying to help you save the dragons?! How dare you pretend—"

"It's not treasure," he mumbled and flopped onto the ground. "It's my heart."

Anna froze. Her eyes dropped to the black gem in her hands. "I don't understand," she said, looking at the heart. "If you left to give it to a dame, then why would you bring it back here?"

Hiro laid his head on the cold ground and covered his eyes with his front claws. He heaved a great sigh, then rolling his shoulder, he said, "Because it broke for you."

Anna started to laugh but stopped herself short. "Is that even possible?" Her tone couldn't hide her disbelief.

He pulled his claws away to peek at her. "The evidence is in your hands."

Without warning, the heart bounced off his ribs. "Hiro, stop this," Anna said with her fists on her hips.

He picked up the heart with his back claw and hefted it back into her belly. "Stop what?" he growled.

After doubling over again from the force of the throw, Anna pursed her lips. "Stop this pretense and tell me what you were really doing." She threw the heart back at his belly, this time with more force.

Now Hiro stood. He picked up the heart, stepped over to the woman and, making sure he steadied her from behind with his opposite claw, punched the heart into her belly. He didn't want to hurt her, but it was somewhat embarrassing having his own heart thrown back at him.

"If you don't believe me," he said, returning to a seated position, "tell me to do something." He sat staring at her, sitting on his hind legs like an obedient pet. The idea made his stomach turn, but he didn't move.

With her fingers wrapped around his heart, Anna tightened her mouth. "Fine," she huffed. "If you want to continue this little game, I'll play along." She licked her lips and looked down at the heart.

"Hiro," she said clearly, "stand up."

Hiro's eyes twitched toward her. Anna's eyes widened and Hiro looked down to see that he was on his feet.

"No," she shook her head, "that one was too easy." She looked around for inspiration. "What can I say to make you prove this heart doesn't belong to me?" She said it more to herself. Then her eyes lit up. With a devious grin on her face, she whispered, "Hiro…cry."

Emotions flooded Hiro's mind and heart. His father's death. The death of several dragons. The recent disappointment and pain on Priya's face. But the foremost thought was the one that he would never be with Anna. They would live separate lives even if she did accept his heart. He would see her rarely and he would never have hatchlings. A stark thought of returning to his cold cave in The Rock Clouds utterly alone assaulted him. Several tears leaked freely from his eyes.

Inside the tears, Hiro saw images. He saw himself fleeing through dark woods away from Noble Guardsmen. He saw Prak, in what seemed to be a war, band alongside Ashel and several other centaurs. Then he saw Anna. A look of solemn, reluctant sorrow on her face as she stood before crowds of people within Kingstor Castle. She was dressed in blue with a long blue veil covering her face and head. A ribbon was tied to her wrist. The other end of the ribbon passed from Philip's hand to the hand of a man old enough to be her father. Philip tied it to the older man's wrist. Philip glanced up at Anna with deepest regret.

Anna squeaked and fumbled the heart in her hands. It fell into the snow at her feet. As Hiro's tears ceased spilling, Anna curled her empty hands around her own shoulders. She stared at the heart in the snow. "Hiro," she whispered looking down at the heart, "you love me."

He didn't answer. He lay back down on the snow and sat staring into the fire beside her.

Anna gingerly bent to pick up the heart. "It's still warm," she said, wiping melted snow from it.

Hiro nodded, "You'll always have my heart and my heat to comfort you."

"What do we do now?" she whispered, still inspecting the heart.

Hiro shook his head. "Nothing," he answered. Anna finally met his eyes. So beautiful. So tender. "I won't ask you if you return the sentiment, because it doesn't matter. I won't ask you to love me, because it won't make a difference. I only ask two things."

Anna took a step toward him. "Anything."

He nodded his head toward her hands. "Keep it. It won't be of use to anyone else, so you should have it."

"And the second?"

"Don't tell anyone. Ever." Their eyes met. "It would only bring more danger to yourself and anyone else. No one can know."

Anna nodded and rolled the teardrop-shaped black heart into her chest. "Hiro," she said, looking down at it again, "I'm still cold."

Hiro reclined onto his side and lifted his front leg and his wing. Keeping her eyes down, Anna curled under them, the precious heart curled in her arms.

——

When he felt Anna began to stir beneath his wing, Hiro lifted it slightly so as not to allow too much cold air in at once. "Are you feeling better?" he asked in a hushed tone.

Anna sat up, pushing herself past the shelter of his wings. "Yes," she answered. Pulling her cloak tight around her shoulders, she stood and walked toward the fire. She started past it but paused. Tilting her head, she asked, "Did you keep the fire going all night?"

"Just in case you needed it," he said. It was a lie. Halfway through the night, while Anna slept, he had felt the fire in his belly gutter, attempting to extinguish again. He silently lit the fire in front of them then and again once the sun came up, for the same reason. He had no idea what to make of his own waning fire and he didn't want to bother her with the problem.

Anna shrugged and stepped into the trees for privacy for her human habit. While she was away Hiro realized that the thought of what she might be doing didn't bother him as much as it had before. When she came back, she sat between Hiro and the fire with her back to the dragon.

Pulling another chunk of meat from her bag, she took a bite. "How far away do you think they are now?"

"They must be several days ahead of us by now," Hiro answered. "I think the faeries must be helping them move at a faster pace. That's why we haven't caught up to them yet."

"Perhaps we should fly for a day," Anna said between bites, "maybe even two."

Hiro nodded. "I think we will."

Anna looked over her shoulder at him. "Just like that? No argument? No million-and-one reasons why we shouldn't possibly do as I suggest?"

Hiro rolled his eyes away from her.

She sighed and turned back to the fire. "I guess having your heart has its advantages."

Hiro took a deep breath. His fire guttered again but continued to burn. "I said we would fly, but I didn't say in which direction."

"Ah," Anna nodded her head, "and please tell me, oh wise dragon, why we're going to leave off our pursuit of the only humans that could possibly tell us what my brother is planning against the dragons?"

"It's too dangerous for you."

Her chin dropped to her chest. "Dangerous for me? What about you?"

"I'll come back later," he said, but a tickle in his throat brought his attention to the fire in his middle dimming. He coughed little spits of fire and his fire grew and glowed as usual.

How often will I have to deal with this? he wondered to himself. *Am I dying?*

When he stopped coughing, he saw Anna kneeling in front of him with concern on her brow. "Are you alright?" she asked.

"I'm fine," he lied again, sitting up on his back legs. "Are you ready to leave?"

Her eyes glanced down at her bag sitting next to her. "You know," she said, allowing some mischief to enter her voice, "I could make you tell me the truth."

He snatched up her bag before she could reach for it. He had felt her moving under his wings. He knew the reason the bag was a little heavier. "We don't have time for that," he snapped. "I should've had you home and been back to the Rock Clouds by now."

She tightened her lips and held out her hand for her bag. Once he returned it to her, she strapped it across her back. "I agree," she said, once it was secure. "We don't have time to bicker and it's too dangerous, for *both* of us, to go any further north right now." She punched her fists on her hips and glared the dragon in the eye. "We should go investigate the other trail. The one leading into the mountains."

Hiro's eyes swung to the bag around her shoulder, "Will you force me?"

She grinned. "Only if I have to."

He rolled his shoulder and scooped her into his fist.

23

HOSTILE ALLIANCES

They reached the diverging path much sooner than Hiro thought possible. He could feel the warmer spring air while flying south and, already knowing their course, the terrain did not slow them. He flew low and close to the trees as they carefully passed the Ice Ruck. Halfway through the next day, they found the trail leading into the mountains.

Hiro flew north of the track without setting down. He didn't want humans to find their tracks into the mountains. Since the snow had mostly melted this far south, his previous tracks had disappeared, and he didn't want to imprint new ones.

"Smoke," he said, spotting it not long after they flew into the mountain range.

"I see it," Anna answered, keeping her voice as low as she could.

The sun, although still up, had dropped behind the trees. Hiro flew to the northern side of the smoke columns and set himself down. Not just one but two fires burned within the trees. Anna climbed cautiously from his claw and tip-toed closer. Hiro crept behind her, taking shelter behind a large stone outcrop.

Anna peered around a thick pine tree. "Can you see anything?" she whispered without taking her eyes from the encampment.

Hiro stifled a growl at his inept night vision. "No," he said, "just the fires. I don't see any movement. I hear very little and all I can smell is…" he growled low.

"What?" she whispered. "What do you smell?"

Hiro licked his fangs. "Men," he lied to her again, "human men." But the tangy smell of flarote almost overpowered every other scent.

"Well, we won't learn anything from this far away." Anna stepped around the tree almost in plain sight of the buildings, but Hiro dragged her back behind the outcrop.

"What are you doing?" he growled.

"I'm going down there," she growled back.

"You are not." He planted her on her backside next to the large boulder. "I'll go see what I can find out."

"Are you crazy?" Anna scrambled to her feet. "You're too big! You'll be seen! I can get in close, peek in some windows, and come straight back here without anyone knowing I was there."

"Not if you make as much noise as you're making now." Hiro began to creep closer to the buildings. His eyes scanned the trees and the grounds around the buildings, but he didn't see anything. "They don't seem to be guarding it very well," he said, searching the trees.

"Well, they wouldn't need to, would they?" Anna's answer came from in front of him. Hiro jerked his head to look at her, wondering how she had gotten in front of him without his notice. "They don't think dragons will come looking for this place, and any humans that come upon them aren't a threat." She shifted her gaze from the buildings back to Hiro. "Which is exactly my point. If anyone catches me snooping, I can just say I was lost in the mountains. If you're caught snooping, they'll put guards out and wonder why a dragon would be sneaking around like a scout cat." She lowered her voice as Hiro's head lowered to her level. "Scout cats are clever, but still just animals. And dragons are nowhere near that smart. At least that's what humans think."

Hiro set his mouth. "Don't be seen," he forced through his clenched jaw.

As Anna flitted down the hill, Hiro realized how little sound she made. She floated over leaves and branches with the smallest of rustles, which might only have been her dress. Eventually she scooped her skirts higher up her legs as she disappeared into the encampment.

Hiro settled behind the outcrop. He watched and listened for any signs of movement. He saw nothing except once, when he thought he saw movement around the edges of the fire on the far side of the encampment. He heard minor movement within the shelters, but the sounds were very faint. From this distance and with the wooden barriers of the buildings' walls, he couldn't hear any breathing or heartbeats. Not even voices would have made it to his ears.

Eventually he hunkered behind the boulder in frustration. When he had almost decided to get up and assist Anna in her search, he heard a familiar rustle behind the rock. Peering around the edge of it, he saw Anna skimming over the sodden ground toward him.

She darted behind the rock and sank to the ground. "It's bad." She shook her head as she gulped a breath. "There's space to house dozens of men at a time. There's a cleared area on the other side that has obviously been used by perhaps a couple hundred men most recently."

"The men we were following."

"Precisely," she continued. "There are at least three faeries down there. Their quarters are stocked with several majikal instruments. There's dozens of men. They don't look exactly busy, more like they're waiting for something right now. But Hiro," she spun to face him with her hands on his claw, "there's a building filled to the rafters with boxes. I can't be certain what's in all of those boxes, but—" she stopped and took a deep breath, "I saw arrows, Hiro. Black-tipped arrows. If all those boxes are full of those poisoned arrows, they have enough to obliterate the Rock Cloud Ruck."

Hiro twisted his neck in the direction of the encampment as if he could see the arrows from there. "Then we have no choice," he mumbled. "I'll have to destroy it."

"Hiro," Anna took a deep breath before she continued, "I agree that it should be destroyed, but going anywhere near it would be too dangerous for you."

His eyes shifted to hers. "I can't leave here without trying. Those arrows could kill every dragon I know."

"I know," she answered quickly, "but maybe you should go get some help. Perhaps Tog will—"

He shook his head. "Tog is too far away. The Rock Clouds are days from here. I'll have to do it myself."

He stood to walk toward the buildings, but Anna jumped in front of him. "Hiro, stop!" she whispered harshly. "You can't do this alone! If only one of those arrows gets nocked—" she couldn't finish the sentence.

"It's a risk I'll have to take," he growled, pushing past her.

"What about the exposure of your intelligence?" she insisted, following him. "A dragon comes out of nowhere and attacks the place where they're secretly storing a dragon poison? Doesn't that seem at all suspicious?"

"That's why I'll have to kill every single human down there," he rumbled.

"But Hiro," Anna ran in front of him, pushing against his chest with her hands, "they have you out-numbered. You can't possible take all of them without one of them getting a shot at you."

"Anna," he growled again, "I have no choice."

"Then I have no choice!" she snapped. Hiro narrowed his eyes and snaked his head to question her. She had her hand in her bag that hung at her hip. She clenched her jaw. "Don't make me force you to get help."

"From whom?" he rumbled. "No one knows I'm here and besides, everyone is too far away to help."

Anna's eyes lit up. "The Ice Ruck."

———

Philip could have melted into those blue eyes and he would have been happy for the rest of his life. Unfortunately, it felt at this moment as if those very eyes would rather smother him.

"I'm sorry, Tierni," Philip tried in vain not to stutter under her piercing gaze. "I'm sorry to have put you in such an awkward position. I didn't realize your relationship to Torgon. Beyond the capacity of servant and king, I'm afraid we won't be able to see much of each other again."

Tierni sighed and dropped her eyes to look at her hands. Her hands hadn't moved from her lap the past few minutes sitting there in the king's office. While he attempted to keep sweat from his forehead by sheer will alone, she hadn't twitched so much as a pinky finger. Her lashes beat a slow, steady patter as he talked himself hoarse of duty, responsibility, and honor. Her lips kept a straight line of indifference as he attempted to brush past any feelings he or she might have for the other. So much so that by the time he finished, he was convinced the feelings were entirely his alone.

"Will that be all, Sire?" she asked, her eyes still lowered.

Philip was struck with an idea that might help him glimpse what was going on in her mind. "If you'd like, I'm sure I could find work for you in another household. A general's home, or one of the Lords' homes, perhaps."

"I don't think that will be necessary," she said, lifting her chin to stare him in the eye. "I enjoy my work in the royal household and you and I have never crossed paths before; I don't see why we should ever cross paths again. I'll be sure to pay better attention to where I wander."

Heaven help any man that tries to resist that gaze! Philip thought to himself.

They both stood in the same movement. "Should I have the guards escort you back?" he asked.

"No need." She swept to the door and swung it open. "I probably know this castle better than you do."

As the door closed behind her, Philip decided to visit the shrine of Tartaku to beg that he see Tierni again. But that would have to come later.

Right on cue, Murthur led Qialla into the office by way of the door leading from the audience hall. The capable servant must have been watching for Tierni to leave by the servant's entry, then led the faerie councilman in by the more distinguished entrance.

Philip tried to straighten his back upon the faerie's entry, but he had a difficult time shaking the memory of Tierni's eyes. "Qialla," he greeted the faerie, waving a hand for him to be seated. But following his own direction as per usual, his hooded head swung only to look at the chair—Philip seethed internally and imagined the faerie's disgusted sneer—and he continued to stand. Outwardly Philip ignored the faerie's rudeness, as he always did. "I trust plans are continuing as you wish."

"Everything is exactly on point, Your Majesty," Qialla said with a nod. "We currently have about half the needed supply of poisoned arrows to attack an entire ruck. We will have the rest within the week. Soon we'll have fliers delivering the supply to everyone who needs it. It is time for you to mobilize your army. We will attack the Rock Cloud Ruck in just more than a month and wipe the—"

"So soon?" Philip barely noticed the sound of his own teeth grinding.

After a short pause Qialla took a small step forward. "Yes, your army shall be at the base of the Rock Clouds in just a few short weeks. The poisoned arrows will be in every quiver of every human and faerie. We will build and majikally enhance large platforms to carry humans into the Rock Clouds. It will be a swift victory."

"The dragons won't stand a chance," Philip mumbled, looking down at his desk.

"But the rest of the species of Avonoa will."

Philip shook his head and closed his eyes. "Are you sure this is the right course of action, Qialla?"

"What are you asking me?"

Now Philip glared into the dark cowl of the faerie's cloak. Perhaps it was the disappointment and frustration over Tierni, but Philip was at his breaking point. Etiquette be damned. "I mean to ask you if you feel in your heart that killing these animals is the right thing to do? Have you no conscience?"

"Those animals are the most dangerous creatures in this world." Qialla's voice rose with every word. "They are a blight on this land and—"

"Yes," Philip nodded, placing his hands on his desk, "they're dangerous. So are scorrands, lions, banshees, worms—even a unicorn could stab you with its horn!" His voice rose to match Qialla's.

Qialla leaned across Philip's massive desk, "A unicorn wouldn't hunt you down because you tried to kill it!" he yelled.

"But to wipe out an entire species!" Philip yelled back. "It's merciless! Who's next, Qialla? Banshees, for feeding their young with your carcass? Scorrands, for protecting their eggs? Centaurs, for just being your enemies?! Where does it stop?!"

"With you!" Qialla barked back. "It stops with you! Whether you help us or not, we're going to kill every dragon across every land! If you don't help us, the killing stops after we've destroyed every single human!"

Philip blinked. He leaned away from the faerie. "An alliance formed of threats is not an alliance; it's slavery."

Qialla leaned back as well. Even though Philip could spit on the top of the faerie's head, it felt as if the faerie towered over him. "The Faerie Council doesn't care how we get your help, only that it is secured."

Philip tried to breath, but it came in shallow gulps. He felt his back against an implied wall. Yes, humans far outnumbered faeries, but the faeries' wings and their majik gave them more strength than any human could imagine.

"If you are quite finished complaining," Qialla said, "I will tell you that the Honorable Kingdom and the Courageous Kingdom are already on their way with their armies to the Rock Clouds. If you won't help us, perhaps you would be willing to assure your fellow humans are not slaughtered by dragons." When Philip didn't answer, Qialla leaned toward him again, but this time he kept his voice to a low hiss. "You will assemble and mobilize your army to the Rock Clouds. If you're too much of a coward, I will lead them there myself."

Philip lifted his chin as high as he could without making it look like he was accepting orders, which it felt like he was. "They've already begun arriving from the outlying counties. We will begin the march west from Kingstor in three days."

24

ESSENTIAL ASSISTANCE

"They'll kill you."

Anna pursed her lips. "Didn't you say that Rakgar made me exempt from that rule?"

"Yes," Hiro sighed. "Rakgar has no authority over the Ice Ruck. If you come with me, they'll kill you first and ask me questions afterward."

Hiro had carried Anna back to the point where the trail diverged, then followed it slightly north to the point closest to the Ice Ruck. They slipped into the trees closest to the edge of the Ice Waste separating the Ice Ruck from the humans' tracks leading north. In the sunlight he could see the mountain home of the ice dragons in the distance. It would take him less than a half day to fly there.

"Follow the trail going south," he told Anna. "You should reach the faerie forest or come upon other humans soon enough."

Anna glanced down at her bag. "And if I make it that far? What then? If I make it home, what do I tell Philip?"

"I've thought about that," Hiro nodded. "You'll have to tell him that you escaped somehow."

"Escaped?" Anna snorted. "Escaped how?"

"I don't know, maybe…" Hiro looked around for some inspiration then struck on an idea. "Flarote," he whispered. He stared at some spring mushrooms sprouting under a thick Plasyte tree, then quickly looked back at Anna. "Tell him you saw smoke and the dragon started acting strangely. Tell him that I dropped you and ran off. You've been trying to find your way back ever since."

"Why?" Anna pressed. "What does it mean?"

Hiro rolled his shoulder. "I smelled some flarote at the encampment. Perhaps they were just using it for their animals, but maybe you could lie and say that the scent of it drove me away. Maybe the scent of it was too strong and it confused me."

Anna nodded. "I suppose that could work. It's better than nothing."

Anna scooped up her belongings. As she turned to search for a clear path through the sparse trees around them, Hiro felt the familiar gutter in his stomach. It lurched and twisted. The waning fire in his belly clenched on his stomach like a giant claw. If he waited much longer his flame would extinguish and he'd die. So, he belched a long burst of flame. Anna spun to face him with wide eyes.

"What was that?" she asked. "Are you alright?"

"I'm fine," he lied again. "I just thought you might like to take some fire with you." He yanked one of the branches from a burnt tree and offered it to her.

She narrowed her eyes at the gift. "I don't think I'll be able to drag that along with me. I'll have to make do with my cloak to keep me warm."

Hiro let the branch fall to the ground and stamped out the flame. "Anna," he said, lowering his head to hers, "I'll find you."

She nodded to him and turned toward the path without another word. After she disappeared into the brush, Hiro spread his wings. Bunching his legs under him, he vaulted into the sky.

———

A bluish-gray dragon circled up from the snow-covered mountain in front of Hiro. The horns circling his head and running along his spine showed that the dragon was a dan, but the horns themselves swayed with movement. Curious. The gray dan looped around Hiro without removing his inspecting eyes as they both flew toward the small mountain range in front of them.

Each mountain snuggled under a blanket of snow despite the rest of Avonoa thawing from warm spring air. Boulders and stunted trees covered the mountains, but Hiro could also see running stream beds and a melting waterfall. The mountains didn't float in the air like the Rock Clouds, but there were roughly the same number of peaks. Hiro wondered if as many dragons lived in this ruck as did in his.

He tried to ignore the escort until they got close enough to the mountains to see several other dragons in flight. Finally he opened his mouth. "Was that a frozen waterfall I saw back there?" Hiro asked casually.

The gray dragon chuckled. "You are a floater, then."

"My name is Hiro Tekla of the Rock Cloud Ruck," he said before swinging his eyes to meet the dan's. "I need to speak to your leader. It's urgent."

"Shining days, Hiro Tekla," the escort dipped his head. "I am Maggoran. I will take you to Rakdar."

Hiro dropped back, allowing Maggoran to take the lead. He drifted left, further north around one of the smaller mountains. As they flew together Hiro saw six dames take flight in a triangle formation. The lead dame was ice blue, as were two others. One of the dames was yellow-green in color, one was pure white like Visi, and the last was a crystalline purple. Most of the dans he saw peeking from cave mouths or flying with hatchlings were different shades of gray. The only brown dans he saw were so pale in color that they might have been orange dames. But almost every dragon he saw had something akin to feathers in their features.

Flying behind Maggoran, Hiro could see the anomaly of feather-like spikes running down his spine. They also circled around the head like plumage on one of the dames flying in formation. A fledgling flying with his sire seemed perfectly sleek at first, but gave a violent shake in mid-air and his entire body puffed out to twice its size.

"What are they?" Hiro blurted out with enormous eyes at the fledgling's expansion.

Maggoran tilted his head to see what Hiro referred to, then chuckled again. "They're scales, of course," he said.

"Scales?"

"Yes," Maggoran shook his head, sending a rippling wave down his spine. As Hiro peered closer he could see light reflected from the needle-like feathers surrounding his spikes. "Our scales have helped us adapt to the colder environment. They're thicker, but smaller and easier to conform to our bodies. I probably have several thousand more scales than you do. They're also attached at the bottom end of each scale so they can lift away from our hides to help us cool, for when the seasons warm."

"Cool?" Hiro tried to contain his shock. "Isn't it cold here all year?"

Maggoran roared with laughter as he swooped down to a steep canyon between two mountains. The sheer cliffs on the sides of the canyon echoed his laughter. He landed in front of a cave opening with two towering stone pillars at each side. Two large dragons jumped from the rock overhead. They were both gray, but one with dark gray streaks around his head and tail stepped in front of the cave.

"What's so funny, Maggoran?" he asked with a grin.

Maggoran coughed to gain control of himself before answering. "This floater asked if it was cold here all year."

The silent dragon also grinned then bounded back onto the cliff face. The gray-streaked dragon turned his smile on Hiro. "Maggoran is young. He hasn't answered that query as many times as I have." His steel-gray eyes pierced Hiro. "No, it is not always cold here."

Maggoran took a deep breath. "Sormano, Hiro Tekla of the Rock Cloud Ruck wishes to see Rakdar. He says it's urgent."

Sormano dipped his head. "Come, Hiro Tekla." He turned and slipped into the cave behind him.

As Hiro followed, he expected the same chill inside the caves as he felt in the Rock Cloud caves. But when he crossed the threshold, he lifted his head and breathed deeply the warmth that met him. He followed Sormano's tail into the depths, expecting darkness, but was again surprised with a warm green glow.

When his eyes adjusted to the greenish light, he saw a pale purple dragon with tufts around her head and wrapping around her shoulders and withers. Her snout was long and pointed and she stared down it at Hiro from small, angled eyes.

She sat in front of three rock spires from the tops of which issued steam. The rock at the tops of the spires gave off the green glow. Hiro glanced to his side and saw a tiered rock wall wrapping around a small chamber. Every layer of the tier was covered in succulent flarote.

"Hiro Tekla of the Rock Cloud Ruck," Sormano gestured from Hiro to the purple dame, "Rakdar of the Ice Ruck."

"Shining days, Rakdar," Hiro said, dipping his head to the dame.

"Clear skies to you, my friend," Rakdar lowered her head in return. She waved a claw beside her in front of the farthest green rock formation. "Please, make yourself comfortable. We haven't had a visitor from the Rock Clouds in several years."

"What is this place?" Hiro couldn't stop himself from asking. He stepped toward the green rock reaching out a claw to inspect it.

"This is how the Ice Ruck survives such harsh conditions, Hiro." Rakdar slithered backward and to one side to make room for him in front of the glowing rocks. "Several caves in these mountains contain this substance." She scratched the glowing green of the rocks and a glittering powder fell to the cave floor. "From what we can guess, it's a natural byproduct of the steam. It keeps us warm in the harshest of temperatures and makes an ideal growing environment for flarote to keep us healthy."

"I often wondered what would make a dragon choose to remain in the cold," Hiro said with a chuckle.

"We have not just adapted to the cold, Hiro;" she said with a grin, "the conditions of our home sustain us. Why would we leave?"

"Hiro," Sormano spoke up from the side of his leader, "I believe you said your message was urgent?"

Rakdar's head shifted from Sormano to Hiro and back again with narrowed eyes. "Urgent?" she asked. "Is something wrong?"

"Yes, Rakdar," Hiro said, sitting up a little taller, "something is very wrong."

He told her everything he could. He told her of the increasing numbers of dragon deaths and the traps set for them. He told her of the mounting antagonism of the Noble Kingdom against the dragons. He told her of the black-tipped arrows they'd found in the ashes of all the dragons. He gave her the memory of visiting the centaurs and discovering the dragon poison. She hissed when she blinked away the memory.

"What can we do, Hiro?" she growled. "What answers have you discovered?"

"I found an encampment less than half a sun cycle's flight from here." As he spoke he watched anger spread across the faces of the two dragons in front of him. "I don't believe it to be the place where they've made the poison, but it holds hundreds, possibly thousands of the poisoned arrows. They could use them at any time. They could kill hundreds of dragons without a fight."

Sormano jumped to his feet only moments before Rakdar did. "We must destroy it!" he barked.

"Gather every dragon that has passed the Krusible," she growled even louder. "Meet at the Krusible."

Hiro scrambled to follow them out of the warm cave. Sormano bounded out first, roaring orders to the guards outside. Once Hiro stepped out of the entrance, he saw several dragons in flight and more bellowing instructions to others. Word spread so fast that by the time Hiro landed behind Rakdar at the Krusible, dozens of dragons already waited for them.

As they waited for the rest to arrive, Hiro marveled at the similarity and differences between the Ice Ruck Krusible and his own. Their Krusible testing grounds didn't stretch out of the side of the mountain like it did in the Rock Clouds, but sat at the very top of one of the tallest mountains. The brutal winds picked up with the altitude and the waning sun off to their side did nothing to warm them. Rakdar sat atop a stone at the edge of the smooth bowl-like area.

Many dragons asked questions as they arrived, but Rakdar glared at them as if they shouldn't expect any answers from her. When Sormano landed next to her and nodded, she finally parted her narrow maw.

"The humans have created a dragon poison," her voice echoed over the Krusible above absolute silence. "We don't know how, but an arrow tipped with a black substance has killed dragons instantly. There can only be one purpose for such a deadly creation." Many of the dragons in front of her growled. Some postured to pounce, others bared their fangs. "We don't know how or where they produce it, but," she waved a claw at Hiro, "Hiro Tekla of the Rock Cloud Ruck has discovered a storing area. We believe it to be the position from which they plan to distribute it for use."

Several dragons belched flame into the sky at these words. Others roared. Some of the younger dragons seemed frightened, but not many. Most had fire burning in their eyes and throats.

Hiro couldn't help but compare the reaction of the Ice Ruck to the news of a dragon poison with the reaction he had received from his own ruck and leader. Here they sprang into action with fires ablaze! In the Rock Clouds, when Hiro had told Rakgar of the dragon poison, they ended up debating the virtues of humans versus faeries.

"There is only one problem!" Sormano's voice shattered the angry roaring of the ruck. When they all silenced, Hiro noticed Rakdar already nodding at Sormano. "If we attack, we run the risk of exposure. The humans might wonder why we would mount an attack on that particular area."

Many dragons ceased their fires, looking to their leaders for guidance and decision. Rakdar nodded, "I believe it's a risk we'll have to take."

"There's no risk," Hiro spoke to Rakdar before turning to address the ruck. "I have information—from a source I can't reveal—that the humans will be told that the smell of flarote drives dragons to near insanity. It will justify an attack."

"I'm beginning to like you, floater," Sormano chuckled.

Rakdar sat up straight. "Either way, we must minimize human survivors. Watchers!" she barked over the ruck. Several dans lifted their heads. "You'll encircle the encampment, slaughter any who try to flee. Come get the information from Hiro."

Maggoran stepped forward. "Tell me where to go, floater."

Hiro passed Maggoran the information of how to get to the encampment and what it looked like as he had seen it. Once he received the memory, Maggoran blinked and squinted at Hiro, but turned without question and gave the information to the other Watchers.

As the Watchers nodded to each other, they then nodded to Rakdar and lifted into the air without another word. Once they were safely away, Rakdar spoke again. "I'll lead whomever wishes to follow. Stakkid, I want you and your huntresses in front with me."

It took Hiro a moment to realize that they were all staring at him. "Hiro," Rakdar stretched out her wings, which looked more like feathers than scales. "Lead the way."

25

OBLITERATION

The Ice Ruck was definitely smaller than the Rock Cloud Ruck. Hiro swept through the icy air with Rakdar on his right flank and Sormano on his left, but only a couple dozen dragons followed behind them. It was possible that others had decided it was too risky to be involved, but Hiro wouldn't believe that. Rakdar led this ruck with ice in her heart and her eyes. Her dragons would be willing to die if she told them to, because she was willing to do the same.

In silence, the large group soared over the barren ice land between the Ice Ruck Mountains and the northernmost Torthoth range. Once in sight of the canyon containing the path to the encampment, Hiro tilted his head to Rakdar. "The buildings are just through—"

He stopped short from a sharp snap of Rakdar's jaws just beside his wing joint. Her frozen blue eyes drilled into his when he met them. Of course. Far beyond the safety of the Ice Ruck's borders, Rakdar wouldn't tolerate any small slip. Hiro should have known better than to speak. He began to wonder about the efficacy of his own Krusible test, and about Anna's influence on him.

Chiding himself internally, he pressed his wings and flew further between the mountains. He could see the path below through the trees. The sun dipped behind the group, but trees towering over the buildings disguised the descending dragon shadows. A single human stood in front of one of the two fires that burned as tall as the man. He only had time for a short scream before Sormano landed, putting one claw through his chest and the other in the flames.

The dragons set to work on the buildings, tearing at them with their claws and searing them with flame. Half a dozen men erupted from one of the buildings. A few of them held swords; the rest held bows with arrows half-nocked. The closest arrow buzzed past Rakdar and two of the huntresses tore the man in half before he could scramble to obtain another arrow. The three men with swords charged Maggoran, but three huntresses stepped beside him. The four dragons raked the men aside with their claws, leaving behind only human shreds.

Hiro perched atop the middle and largest building, tearing at the wooden pieces holding it together, when he caught the scent. Lighter and leafier green than a human's animal-like scent, it made him whip his head around. With barely a moment to lose, Hiro tumbled horn-over-tail to the ground as a poisoned arrow whistled past him. Unfortunately, the arrow sliced the upper front leg of the gray dan behind Hiro, instantly turning him to ash.

Maggoran saw the attack and bellowed before launching himself at the creature who sent the killing dart. Skorkot, her cloak's hood thrown back to face the dragons, lowered her bow but lifted her chin at the challenge. As Maggoran hurtled toward her, she reached into her robes and withdrew a puff of powder to throw into Maggoran's face moments before his fangs reached her throat. Once the powder hit the dragon, Skorkot stepped aside and let the unconscious mass flop next to her.

Her black eyes swung to meet Hiro's again. But Hiro knew better than to engage her immediately. She inched closer to the building's edge. She didn't want to use the powder on Hiro. He knew her. He could tell Rakgar. He *would* tell Rakgar. Her finger twitched toward the corner of the building. Her eyes locked with his. Hiro knew she hoped to distract him from her fingers creeping toward the unseen edge of the building. There must be something behind it that she desperately wanted to use on the black dragon.

Three other dans saw Maggoran lying on the ground. Hiro guessed that they assumed he was dead, but Hiro knew better. That powder had been used on him before. It could render a dragon unconscious in a blink, but it wasn't lethal. While the others attacked Skorkot, Hiro held back.

As anticipated, she threw handfuls of the non-lethal powder in all of their faces. When the last unconscious dragon slammed into the building wall in front of her, blocking Hiro's view, Skorkot disappeared. Hiro crawled backward from where the faerie had stood, stepping two claws into the burning fire. Wrapping his talons around a clump of embers, he scanned the trees around them, waiting.

He didn't have to wait long. The faerie shot out from behind the building straight into the sky. The poisoned arrow nocked. But Hiro couldn't move until she did first. With a scream, she dove over the building through the flames now licking the walls. Once she burst through them, Hiro rolled to the side, casting a clawful of scalding embers into the faerie's face. She screamed again as the arrow in her bow loosed harmlessly into the shadows of the trees.

Hiro plucked the treacherous faerie from the air and pinned her to the ground. He slowly sunk his talons into the soft flesh of her chest. Her wailing waned as a handful of dragons gathered around them. Some roared—Hiro wasn't sure if their anger was directed toward him or the faerie, but he didn't care. His claw contracted around the faerie's heart.

Her screaming stopped, but her eyes lifted to Hiro. With blood dripping from her lips, she whispered, "Every dragon must die."

Her limbs contorted, her back tried to arch, then she lay still.

Rakgar will see this, Hiro swore in the back of his mind. *By Khurta's claws, he can't ignore it.*

———

The screaming and moaning coming from the human men faded with the last rays of light. Rakdar and the huntresses roared over the embers of four dragons lost. Maggoran and the others lay still on the ground.

A few of the other dragons nudged them with their snouts and wailed a lament. Hiro longed to relieve their suffering. He knew they thought the stunned dragons would be cursed in The World of Souls because they hadn't been burned to ash, but he didn't dare say a word. He knew the worst that could happen would be that the unconscious dragons would wake after everyone had gone and would return home later.

Hiro, however, continued digging through piles of charred timbers. He tore down remaining walls and burned everything he touched. The other dragons sometimes helped, but most watched. When he found a round container stuffed full of black-tipped arrows, he burnt it so hot that the metal rings around the outside glowed white. When the others saw the contents, they joined him to search for more.

Altogether they found eight of the circular containers crowded in different shelters. While the outside of the containers burned normally, the black tips of the arrows continued burning longer than the arrows themselves. Once the black tips turned as red as blood, the fire finally would sputter out. Rakdar watched the small fires dwindle. Every last one.

Hiro found himself scratching at the bottom mudwork of one of the last buildings. There wasn't much more than scorch marks left covering the entire area. When he realized he would find nothing else, he stepped back and took a deep breath.

The faint scent of human sweat drifted to his nose on a breeze.

Hiro's eyes narrowed. It was definitely a human scent. Everything with a human scent should have been burnt at that point. His eyes scoured the ground, but in the darkness he couldn't see anything.

He lowered his nose to the ground. Yes, it was human. The scent was stronger further away from the rubble. Hiro walked away from the building, swinging his snout back and forth, sweeping the ground. Sormano stepped beside him. When Hiro tilted his head at the elder dragon, the question was clear in Sormano's eyes.

Hiro lifted his head and placed it in front of Sormano's. With a short burst of warm air, he sent the memory of Rakdar telling the Watchers to surround the encampment and slaughter any humans who tried to escape.

Sormano's eyes narrowed more. He cast a sharp look at Maggoran's still form on the ground. He placed his snout in front of Hiro's.

Sormano had seen the Watchers in the trees. He could see them surrounding the human encampment before the attack began. He could see Maggoran crouching low in the trees directly in front of where Hiro stood now. Maggoran had been on watch here.

Then Hiro remembered. Maggoran had jumped out at Skorkot when she attacked Hiro. Some humans must have slipped by them.

"What happened to them?" Sormano's voice was so quiet, Hiro was surprised he could even hear the question. Rakdar ran a very tight ruck indeed. "Are they cursed?"

Hiro shook his head. "They will wake."

The scent of human tantalized Hiro's senses. "Some of them escaped," he told Sormano, matching the almost silent tone. "I can smell them."

Sormano gave Hiro the memory of Rakdar saying they must minimize survivors. He repeated the word "minimize." Hiro understood. He was explaining that they might not get them all.

But Hiro knew they were more of a danger than any of these dragons understood. Any survivors would get information to Philip. Any survivors might find Anna. Any survivors might refute her stories of the dragons.

He growled to himself. He couldn't use memory to explain this to Rakdar. He searched into the trees and smelled the human scent getting stronger as he followed it. It led him past the scent of dragons around the encampment. There were definitely survivors.

Galloping back into the scorched encampment, Hiro skidded to a halt in front of Rakdar. Huntresses and Watchers were spreading their wings and lifting into the sky.

"Survivors," he whispered as low as he could. "I caught their scent further into the trees than the Watchers—" He cut himself off at her sharp snarl but didn't give up. "They might make it back to other humans—" She growled louder. "You must help me hunt them down."

His whisper had become louder than he realized. Rakdar roared into his face. Putting her nose in front of Hiro's, she breathed a series of memories. In each one, she roared the same word. "ENOUGH!"

Hiro cringed. Rakdar's feathers stood out on her neck and body. As beautiful as he had found her before, she was even more terrifying now. She shook out her feathery wings. Roaring, she vaulted into the sky. The rest of the ruck rose with her. Hiro watched as they melted into the thick darkness.

26

NARROW ESCAPE

Torgon's heart pounded as he leapt through the trees. Darting behind another large boulder, he spun around to ensure the other five men with him reached the rock for safety. His heart continued to thud against his ribs and he wondered for the millionth time if his father had ever felt such fear in the face of danger.

Torgon grabbed the shoulder of the last man through. "You're sure there were no other survivors in your barracks?" he asked again.

"No, General," the breathless man whispered back, "I watched them die."

Torgon had only arrived the day before and planned to leave the next morning to go to The Great Northern Mountain. He had been alone in his room, the only other private room besides the one the faerie had taken, when the dragons attacked the outpost. Grateful he hadn't yet undressed for the night, he'd rushed to the other buildings to help men escape or fight. He remembered watching the men being struck down and decided that a swift and quiet escape was their only option.

The attack was vicious. In his twenty years Torgon had never seen a dragon act this way. The only sightings he'd had as a child were when a dragon would occasionally fly overhead. He never saw one up close until after his father's death. Even seeing the aftermath of that attack hadn't prepared him for the brutal attack tonight.

"Where did they come from, General?" one of the men whispered between shaky breaths. He bore the lieutenant's symbol of swords on his tunic. The rest of the men were staff guards. None of them wore a sword on their hip, which meant only he and the lieutenant could handle one.

"Why did they attack the outpost?" another man asked. When Torgon glanced up at the man who was easily more than a decade his senior, the man trembled.

They're just as afraid as I am, Torgon realized. *Despite my own fear, I'm their leader. If I show fear, they will falter.*

"I don't know," Torgon answered, relieved his voice didn't quake. He took a deep breath. "We need to make our way back to Kingstor. There should be a vill—"

He briefly froze, then turned to peer around the boulder. Every muscle in his body tensed. Something was out there. The men, sensing their leader's tension, froze too. In the back of his mind Torgon wondered if they were even still breathing.

"We need to move," he whispered, turning back to them. He pointed behind them. "Get behind those boulders." He turned back to peer into the darkness. "Now."

———

Hiro really couldn't begrudge Rakdar leaving. Rakdar had done what she said she would. In fact, with this act of leadership against the humans, she had done more for her ruck than Rakgar had done for his. No dragon had spoken in front of the humans, so he knew she didn't see the need to slaughter the survivors. Hiro, however, wasn't sure what they would do if they found Anna. Would they question her? Help her? His heart pulled him toward her, but his head told him she would be fine and he should go straight back to the Rock Clouds.

Hiro's nose swept the ground, tracking the human scent. Why couldn't he just let the woman be? Every time he thought of lifting into the air to leave, the image of Anna crumpled under the snow assaulted his mind. He couldn't leave her. He had to make sure she was safe.

He wondered if the human survivors would find her. Perhaps they had already. He certainly couldn't kill them if she was with them. Or maybe he should. Maybe he should take her back to Kingstor Noble himself. She would definitely be safer with a dragon.

He crashed through brush and trees. Stumbled over rocks. Dug his snout through mounds of melting snow. They couldn't possibly be much further ahead of him. They had no faerie with them this time to hurry them on. At least he didn't smell one.

He followed the survivors' trail as it wound sharply to one side and back. He was almost within sight of the road they had first followed north after the men. He assumed the escaped men found the road and were going to follow it back to Kingstor Noble. As he bumbled through bracken, stomping a small bush with yellowish-green buds on the tips he caught a new scent. Anna.

Anna's sweet scent, much more diluted than the men's strong, salty sweat, joined the men's path. Whoever had escaped the attack, had also found Anna. The men's scent turned toward the road. Anna's scent joined theirs. Then all of them clambered back into the trees. Several dragon lengths ahead, piles of boulders huddled at the bottom of a mountain, like pieces of mountain trolls fallen from the cliff behind them. The human scent made an almost straight pathway to them.

Perfect place for an ambush, Hiro told himself as he tip-taloned toward them. *Perhaps I should fly over first.*

He heard a whisper and turned toward the rocks, but stopped and closed his eyes. The forest was quiet. Humans having already passed would've silenced all the night animals. A few crickets chirruped warily then stopped again. He could hear a few small heartbeats of animals waiting in their burrows for the dangerous animals outside to pass. He crept along.

———

Although he had barely breathed it, the men heard and obeyed Torgon's order to move. One by one, they bolted from the boulder they had huddled behind toward the larger group of rocks he indicated. He counted them off as they scurried away. Once the last one slipped behind the large rocks, he followed.

He surveyed the men again. He had his sword on his hip, two of the staff guards had staffs, and the lieutenant had a long dagger on his belt. One of the staff guards clutched three poisoned arrows in his fist. Staring at the shivering men Torgon pulled his sword free of its sheath. "Spit in Tarsa's eye," he cursed. Spitting into the god of the wind's face never is a good idea, but it was the only one left for the men. Fight. Turning back to await whatever was coming for them, Torgon felt the men steel themselves behind him.

—

Hiro could hear larger hearts beating behind the boulders as he got closer. He thought he saw a head peek over the rock, but he couldn't be certain in the darkness.

So they mean to ambush me, he thought. *These humans are braver than I thought. Or stupid.*

He crept closer to the boulders.

One. Two. Three … Six hearts beating. They beat a quick pace, but not the flutter of fear. A steady, solid beat like the sound they made whenever he had attacked humans. These hearts were ready for a fight.

He crept closer.

A breeze sighed through the trees. The scent had changed. Sweat cooled and the scent of fear lessened. The dull scent of power, strength, focus…determination. Not stupid, then.

Hiro thought he heard a whisper. He crept closer, pausing with each step. His belly brushed the ground. His body low in an attack posture. His tail trailed behind him, swinging to steady each step.

As he paused, he thought he saw movement at the edge of his vision. He froze in place, but flicked his eyes to the side. He couldn't see anything in the darkness. The hearts continued beating steadily on the other side of the boulders, so he chanced turning his head toward the movement.

———

It only took a few moments. The black dragon poured like a shadow between the trees.

Why is it always that same dragon? Torgon wondered to himself. He peered between the rocks as the beast slithered in the direction the group had followed. Step for step, he covered the very ground the men had just abandoned.

"He must be following our scent." Torgon didn't realize he'd spoken until the dragon turned in their direction.

Fool! he chastised himself. *Keep your head about you or you'll get these men killed!*

———

As he snaked his long neck away from the scent trail of the men, he breathed in deeply. Anna. Her scent diverted to the side of where the men prepared their last defense. Hiro's head lifted ever so slightly as he peered into the trees and rocks where he thought he had seen the movement. Was it her? Had she run off in another direction? Away from the men?

He didn't want to risk engaging the men if her scent led somewhere else. Without another glance back at the boulders, Hiro tore into the trees where Anna's scent led. He followed it further into the trees, but the scent snaked to the north. He skidded to a halt. He was following her old scent and going in the wrong direction!

Stupid worm! he chided himself. The humans must have seen the road and decided to stay hidden in the forest. Their paths must have crossed, but Anna headed in the other direction long before the men came that way. Hiro adjusted his direction and ran toward where he knew the road must be, knowing he could follow it and find Anna's scent again further south.

—

Torgon ducked his head and kept it low as the monster drew closer. He couldn't hear it. Not a sound. He waited motionless before he dared peek out again.

His eyes narrowed as he watched the dragon's head swing to the side. Its head lifted. With no more noise than a sigh, the dragon suddenly tore off away from them, deeper into the trees.

Torgon released the breath he'd been holding, but continued to stare, bewildered, after the dragon.

"General," one of the men behind him said, "should we retreat further? Royal General Torgon?"

The man's urgent tone brought Torgon back to himself. "Yes," he nodded, still staring after the black monster. "Lieutenant, lead the way further south."

As the men behind him disappeared into the darkness, Torgon shook his head in the direction the threat had just departed. "That dragon isn't right."

27

ENIGMAS

He found her scent along the road. If the human men hadn't been afraid to use the road, they might have found her eventually. But Hiro found her quicker. He followed her trail as she had stumbled along the road, taking shelter under trees, scuffing her feet along the pathway, even, at times, crawling on her hands and knees.

He finally found her huddled under a huge pine tree. Lying on a bed of pine needles, her breathing was ragged and she shook from the cold.

"I couldn't find you," she muttered in her delirium. "I just couldn't walk anymore."

Hiro scooped her into his front legs. Using the open space of the roadway, he lifted into the air. He didn't have to take her far to find a protected clearing where he could set down. He ripped down a tree next to them and poured his fire over it. He curled around Anna lending her his own warmth and the warmth of the fire. After just a few minutes, she stirred again.

When she finally looked up at him, he said, "Your hair looks like a nest of fighting younglings." She grinned and turned away. "When did you eat last?"

"It's been a few days," she answered. "But I need water more than food."

"Why haven't you eaten some of the snow?"

She shook her head. "I did eat a little, but I couldn't take in too much without you near me. Snow is good for water, but it makes a human too cold. I can eat it now." She sat up but slumped back down to the ground. "Maybe I'll get it in a few more minutes."

Hiro rolled his eyes. "Little human," he whispered. He gently set Anna aside. He didn't have to go far for snow. Clumps of it lay scattered around the clearing, although none was close to the fire. He dumped a few handfuls in front of her.

As the night wore on with his warmth beside her, Anna scooped handfuls of snow into her mouth. She sat up a few times but dozed often. Hiro sat curled around her, only moving to fetch more snow after it melted.

When morning broke, no snow remained. Anna sat up tall but didn't get to her feet. "I have to go back, Hiro."

He nodded. "I know roughly where the human men are traveling. I can try to put you in their path."

They sat in silence. Then Anna shook her head. "That facility couldn't have been where they made the poison. It was too small. There were too few men."

"Don't worry about it," Hiro told her. "It's a problem for dragons."

Her stern eyes turned on him. "And who will help you? Your own Rakgar doesn't believe the threat. He listens to the faeries."

Hiro remembered killing Skorkot. The vision of the treacherous faerie burned in his mind. "He'll soon learn not to."

"But I'm the only one who has access to question Philip." She folded her arms across her chest. "I think he's learning to trust me more. I'll do whatever it takes to get any information you need, but…" her voice dropped. "How do I get it to you?"

"You don't," he said, staring into the trees. "I told you, this is not your problem."

"Hiro," her voice was so stern his head snapped to look at her, "I'm your friend. I won't abandon you."

The reminder that he had abandoned her recently almost froze the fire in his belly. He turned away from her face in shame.

How things have changed, he thought to himself. *My heart breaks for a human and I trust her more than I would trust my own Rakgar.*

"I know," she said resolutely, "you'll have to risk coming to see me regularly, perhaps once a week. I'll hang a red banner from my window if we need to meet and speak. I'm sure guards will patrol the borders of the king's lands, but there's a cliff at the base of one of the middle mountains just inside. At the bottom of the cliff is a meadow. I'm fairly certain we can meet there without interruption."

Hiro studied the ground as she spoke, only partially listening to her. *I have changed, true,* he considered to himself, *but the world around me has not. Only my perception of it. If the world has not changed, then perhaps everything is not as I have been taught.*

"Mid-day," she continued, "guards wouldn't expect a dragon to wander into the king's forest at mid-day. I assume you'll be able to see a red banner hanging from my window from the mountains behind the king's forest?"

"I could see a red ribbon tied in your hair on a clear day," he admitted, "but this is too dangerous."

"Are you afraid to meet me?" she asked with a raised eyebrow.

"I don't care how dangerous it is for me." He tilted his head down to meet her eye. "What happens to the trust you've built with Philip if he finds out you're trying to help me?"

Her chest expanded with a deep sigh then she nodded as if coming to a decision. "I think he feels the same way as I do." Hiro's chest rumbled with a chuckle. "No, really," she insisted. "I don't think he desires this hostility with the dragons any more than you or I. He's being forced into it, really. I'm almost sure of it."

"Either way," he said, "your place is with the other humans."

"Will you visit me?" she asked. When he didn't answer her, she placed both hands on his claw. "Please," she pleaded, then sat up straight. "Or do I need to use your own heart against you?"

He growled low and soft, not threatening. "As disgusting as you might still be," he finally relented, "I'll visit you."

28

MISINFORMATION

"I think it was the flarote," Anna said as she reclined on her pillows. Her face had been washed in a long, hot bath, but it didn't improve her appearance. The hollows in her cheeks were more pronounced now that she had been warmed, but pink flowed through her skin again. Philip could see deep purple circles around her eyes as well. Her dress had been discarded as worse than a rag.

The healer and majishun had gone when Philip and Torgon arrived. Anna's maid, Amethyst, sat on the edge of Anna's bed, spooning soup into her mouth when she would take it. The maid's eyes were red and bloodshot. She was in almost as bad a state as her mistress.

The king and his Royal General sat in chairs at Anna's bedside. Philip felt like he was visiting his father on his deathbed again and had trouble sitting still. Except this visit could possibly hold some answers.

"Flarote?" Philip asked, glancing at Torgon.

"After we landed in the cave, I tried to get away, but I couldn't get past the dragon to the front of the cave so I went to the back," Anna continued. "I found a bulb of flarote against the wall and grabbed it, hoping I could distract the dragon with it or something. It chased me to the back and knocked me down and the bulb got squished in my hand. When the dragon reached for me again, I hit it in the nose with my fist full of the squished flarote. I smeared it all over its snout. That's when it went crazy."

"Crazy?" Torgon asked with narrowed eyes. He and Philip shared another glance.

"Yes," Anna's eyes widened. She stared past them. "It thrashed, bumped against the walls, and even sneezed lava! It tried to chase after me, but it acted like its body wouldn't move the way it wanted it to. I was able to run past it to get out of the cave. Once I made it outside, I ran downhill. I hid behind some trees. The dragon finally came out of the cave, but it would run, then flap its wings, then fall. It scratched at its nose a few times too. It flew off and crashed in the trees. I ran south." She finished with a shrug. "It was the strangest thing I've ever seen."

"This could explain a lot," Torgon spoke from Philip's side. All eyes turned toward him. "If the flarote made your dragon crazy enough for you to get away, then why couldn't it have caused the dragon to kill those months ago?"

"Or cause it to attack us in the first place," Philip said, remembering the flarote-based poison the faeries cooked up in the rooms they held in the castle.

Torgon nodded. He and Philip stared at each other. Philip assumed his friend knew they were both referring to the attack on the outpost.

"Wait," Anna said, "what does flarote have to do with either of those events?"

"Who knows?" Torgon sat up straight with an air of indifference. "Maybe the dragon overdosed before them, or maybe that dragon has an inborn side-effect to it. Either way, we can't be sure how it affects other dragons, but at least we know it somehow bothers the black one."

Anna shook her head. "I never said the dragon that captured me was black."

"But the black dragon was seen just a day or two before," Torgon said. "I assumed—"

"It was a red dragon," Anna stated. She slumped into her pillows. Her maid took advantage of her silence to offer more soup. Once she swallowed, Anna added, "she had yellow wing tips."

———

Moments later, Torgon closed the door to Anna's chambers behind himself and Philip. Once the latch clicked in place, they locked eyes.

Torgon broke the silence. "You didn't tell her about the betrothal."

"No need to bother her with that now." Philip waved it aside, then turned and glared at the door as if he wanted to bash it in. "Do you think she's lying?" he asked in a hushed voice.

Torgon shook his head. "To what end?"

Philip's head jerked to face him. "That's not what I asked."

Torgon scrubbed his hands through his hair. "Are you asking me as a friend or as a king?"

"Both," Philip answered. "Give me two answers, if you like."

"As your friend, I'd like you to be able to trust your sister." He scuffed his boot on the floor. "But as your Royal General..."

"There's still something we're missing," Philip finished for him. "Isn't there?"

Torgon tilted his head and met Philip's eye again. "The bit about the flarote makes a lot of sense, but...it did seem somewhat...rehearsed."

"All the poisoned arrows at the outpost were destroyed, correct?" Philip asked.

Torgon nodded. "We made off with a handful, no more."

"Good," the young king folded his arms at his chest. "At least the odds are improving that we won't have another attack soon."

"We can't be certain of it," Torgon added.

"Either way," Philip stalked off down the hall with Torgon in his wake, "this attack on the dragons has been delayed. I intend to make the most of it."

29

THE TRUE ENEMY

Hiro's claws landed a little harder on the lip of Rakgar's cave than he intended. His temper had risen with every wingfall on his course back to the Rock Clouds. The more he thought about the faerie Skorkot and her treachery, the angrier he became.

Why couldn't Rakgar see past the faeries' lies? Why did he trust them so blindly? If Tusten had still been here, would he have listened to him? Why wouldn't he listen to Hiro in his father's stead?

He stalked into the cave, ignoring the questions from The Watch. His neck dipped down as they followed him in growing silence. His body elongated, snaking down the entrance to the large chamber beyond. Rakgar would soon understand. He had to.

He growled low when he entered the chamber where Rakgar waited. The dragons standing nearby turned at the sound. Rakgar looked up from the opposite side of the dragons grouped around him. Mitashio sat on his left. He raised one scaly eyebrow at Hiro but did nothing more. Several other dragons sat or lay curled on the stones around Rakgar but Hiro ignored them all, except two.

Tog rounded the group then stumbled over to Hiro a little slower than the small brown dragon ahead of him. Prak's nasal voice began with the questions.

"Hiro, where have you been? We didn't think it would take you this long! Did you run into trouble, Hiro? Are you alright? Did the humans attack you again? I knew I should have gone along with you! Did the human give you any trouble? Did it try to run away? Did you eat it? I would have eaten it! Rakgar said she was nothing but a nuisance the entire time she was here! I know it was just a short time, but any human would be trouble! Did she give you any trouble? Did you just kill her? I probably would have just killed her."

When Prak took a breath, Tog interjected, "Yes, where have you been?"

Hiro ignored Prak's prattling and eyed Tog, "Getting proof." He glared directly at Rakgar and shouldered past his friends.

Hiro could hear Prak whispering questions to Tog behind him, but he snaked his way to Rakgar.

"Hiro," Rakgar sat up straight. Since he sat up so much taller than Hiro, the black dragon was forced to stop directly under the large gray dragon's intimidating eye. "Did you have any trouble with your mission?"

"Indeed, Rakgar," Hiro said loud and clear for the whole chamber to hear. "Do you want me to explain it to you now, or would you rather receive my memories?"

A choice, Hiro thought. *Does he want everyone to hear this or will he try to keep it secret?*

Rakgar's face could have been stone. Finally, he bent his neck to place his nose in front of Hiro.

Hiro gave him the memory of Rylan telling him of the dragon poison. Next, seeing the outpost from a distance. His time in the Ice Ruck. The anger of the Ice Ruck at the human danger. He sent that memory twice, hoping his leader would see the sense in their reaction. The memory of destroying the encampment. Last, he sent the memory of Skorkot trying to kill him with the poisoned arrow.

When Rakgar blinked the memories away, Hiro opened his mouth to speak, but Rakgar was faster. He blew a memory into Hiro's face. It was brief. It had obviously been received from another dragon, but the message was that of Rakgar standing in front of the sender.

"Speak of this to no one. Give none this memory."

Hiro blinked. Rakgar was trying to hide the truth. Why?

"Will you still defend them?" Hiro growled.

"Hiro," Rakgar barked a warning. "Not everyone should know this." The massive grey dragon lowered his voice even more. "Maybe something should be done, but we can't incite panic."

Hiro narrowed his eyes. He had never been the obedient type. "Dragons don't panic. Did the Ice Ruck panic?" he asked. He swung a claw at the others in the cave.

"They have a right to know who their enemies truly are!" His voice rose with every word. He spun away from Rakgar to face the dragons in the cave. "The faerie, Skorkot, tried to kill me! As did the faeries Kradik and Ortym. I will never trust a faerie again!" he whipped his head to Rakgar. "And neither should you."

He loped from the great cavern alone. The only sound in his wake was the clacking of his claws against the stone.

———

Priya landed on the clifftop, stumbling slightly. Visi, as always, sat waiting. The only part of her moving was her tail, lazily lifting and flopping back to the ground.

"Well?" the old, white dragon asked without looking at her companion.

Priya settled back on her haunches. "It happened just like you said it would."

"You doubted?"

"Of course not," the young green dragon said. "I just…hoped."

"Now you understand the delicate balance of the future and what we wish to accomplish." Visi didn't make it a question. She rarely asked questions.

"I've always understood," Priya said. "I just wish there were an easier way."

Visi sighed. "Let me see it."

Priya tilted her head away. "You doubt?"

Visi lifted herself from the ground to take steady steps toward the young dame. "Let me see it," she enunciated each word slowly.

Without looking at the elder dragon, Priya lifted her claw. Under her hovering talons glittered a midnight black, teardrop-shaped dragon heart.

THE END

The adventure continues in…

THE TRAITOR OF AVONOA

Book Four in the Avonoa series

Note to Readers!

I hope you are enjoying the adventure in Avonoa as much
as I enjoyed creating it! Although I love to write and
create these stories, being an independent author is hard.
I don't have teams of people ghost-writing, editing,
formatting and marketing for me. I do it all on my own,
so my only support comes from readers like you! Thank
you for supporting me and my craft.

Another way you can support a lowly indie author like
myself is to leave me a review. Feel free to use the link
above to let others know how much you enjoyed the
story and you can pick up the next book at the same time!
Enjoy the adventure!!

You can also sign up for my newsletter to be the first to
hear about sales, signing events and new books! Sign up
at avonoa.com, hrbcollotzi.com, or
peopleofthestorm.com.

Or follow me on social media…
Facebook @hrbcollotzi
Instagram @hrbcolloti

THE TRAITOR OF AVONOA

Embodiment of Betrayal!

He can't trust anyone…especially himself!

The extinction of dragons has never been more imminent as human armies, equipped with the faeries' dragon poison, surround the Rock Clouds.

While dragons fight amongst themselves, Hiro's body rages within him. Even with the centaurs' help, everyone knows it won't be enough. Hiro is desperate for the survival of the dragons. Unfortunately, he can't even save himself.

9 781962 628167